Suddenly Supernatural

CROSSING OVER

by
Elizabeth Cody Kimmel

LITTLE, BROWN AND COMPANY

New York Boston

Little, Brown and Company

Hachette Book Group
237 Park Avenue, New York, NY 10017
Visit our website at www.lb-kids.com

Little, Brown and Company is a division of Hachette Book Group, Inc.
The Little, Brown name and logo are trademarks of Hachette Book Group, Inc.

The publisher is not responsible for websites (or their content)
that are not owned by the publisher.

First Paperback Edition: October 2011
First published in hardcover in May 2010 by Little, Brown and Company

The characters and events portrayed in this book are fictitious. Any similarity to real persons, living or dead, is coincidental and not intended by the author.

Library of Congress Cataloging-in-Publication Data

Kimmel, Elizabeth Cody
Crossing over / by Elizabeth Cody Kimmel. — 1st ed.
p. cm. —(Suddenly supernatural ; bk.4)
Summary: Feeling more comfortable with her developing skills as a medium, eighth-grader Kat looks forward to the class trip to Montreal but once there she finds herself confronted by a cast of all new ghosts and a host of other problems.
ISBN 978-0-316-07369-1 (hc) / ISBN 978-0-316-13345-6 (pb)
[1. Spiritualists—Fiction. 2. Supernatural—Fiction. 3. Friendship—Fiction. 4. Mothers and daughters—Fiction. 5 Montreal (Quebec)—Fiction. 6. Canada—Fiction.] I. Title.
PZ7.K56475Cro 2010
[Fic]—dc22   2009040081

10 9 8 7 6 5 4 3 2 1

RRD-C

Printed in the United States of America

Suddenly Supernatural

CROSSING OVER

To the 2009 Haldane School Montreal trip.

Je me souviens!

Chapter 1

So the good news was my best friend Jac and I were both on the school French class trip to Montreal.

The bad news was so were Shoshanna Longbarrow and the super-popular Satellite Girls that orbit her — including Brooklyn Bigelow.

The good news was my mom had come along as a chaperone.

The bad news was my mom had come along as a chaperone.

And the worst news was Jac's mother had also come along as a chaperone.

In the seven or so months since random ghosts and haunters and formerly alive people started materializing in front of me, I'd seen a lot of strange stuff. But I'm not sure any of it could hold a candle to the sight of my mother and Jac's mother together.

My mom favored old hippie clothes and hand-me-downs, would not eat meat or kill an insect no matter how hideous or bitey it was, and helped the dead communicate with the living—an ability she had passed on to me. Jac's mom dressed like she was having lunch at the White House (today she was wearing a pressed pantsuit, a neck scarf, and her ever-present string of pearls), she was tightly wound, and she spent most of her energy trying to redirect her musically gifted daughter back to her cello practicing. In short, our mothers had about as much in common as Justin Timberlake and the Pope.

So far, they were kind of ignoring one another.

"The bathroom smells," Jac said, her face turned toward the window as northern New York went by in a blur.

"Do you think they're ever going to speak to each other?" I asked, staring at the back of my mother's head.

My mother was up front, in the third row of the bus, on the right-hand side. Jac's mom was in the first row on the left-hand side, right behind the bus driver, Tim. Actually, Tim was not a bus driver. He announced before we even got under way that we could call him Tim and that he was a *motor coach operator*. It did have a nice ring to it.

Our French teacher, Mrs. Redd, was in the second row, like a carefully placed ambassador stationed between my mother and Jac's mother. There were two empty rows after that, then me and Jac, in the no-man's land of Middle Bus. Then came a cluster of boys and non-Satellite people. Shoshanna and her worshipful Satellite Girls, none more of a suck-up than Brooklyn Bigelow, had absorbed the back four rows into their personal sparkly orbit.

"I think they kind of have to," Jac said. "They'll need to exchange some sort of chaperone-type information eventually."

"Can you picture it?" I asked, glumly. "Your mom will be all, 'So, what do you do?' even though you know she totally knows, and my mom will be all, 'I facilitate communication between the living and the recently departed,' and your mom will be all, 'You mean people who are relocating to a new area?' and my mom will be all, 'I mean people who are relocating to being dead.' And then your mom will turn white as a sheet and press her lips together the way she does…"

Jac immediately did a perfect imitation of the face.

"Yep, that's it exactly, and then she'll make the bus driver pull over. And she'll get off and stand at the side of the interstate and wait for help to come."

Jac tucked a strand of red hair, which was growing out from a short cut and had entered an awkward stage, behind her tiny ear.

"Or," she said very quietly, "Your mom could go, 'Hey, I'm Jane, Kat Roberts's mom,' and my mom could pretend she has no idea you even have a mom, even though you came to the Mountain House with us over spring break. Then, she'll go, 'I am pleased to meet you, *Mrs. Roberts,* I am *Mrs. Gray,*' but she won't look pleased at all.

"Your mom will go, 'There are two spirits following you that wish to communicate,' and my mom will go, 'Excuse me?' Then, your mom will go, 'Do you know a rather squat man with a thick black mustache and a very strong chin, because I see him at your left elbow,' and my mom will go, 'I'm sorry, I think there's been some sort of confusion,' and she'll turn and face the other direction and never look at or speak to your mom again. At the next rest stop she'll accost me in the bathroom and tell me that I am never, never to associate with you again."

"Nice, Jac," I said. "I think I like my version better."

"I don't like either version," Jac said. "At least you get along with your mom."

"I know," I said. "But Brooklyn Bigelow still thinks my mother is some kind of devil worshipper. Did you see the way she checked out Mom's outfit when we met outside the bus this morning? She totally mouthed the word *puhlease* and made a big show of trying not to laugh."

"I like the way your mom dresses," Jac said. "She looks cute in tie-dye and jeans. My mother looks like she's about to go on *Good Morning America* to discuss manners. I mean, whose mother seriously wears a gingham suit on a school trip?"

"Yours," I said gently.

"Aren't we the dynamic duo of Medford, New York," Jac said. "Jac Gray, on-again off-again cellist, and Kat Roberts, eighth-grade radio to the dead."

"And our mothers, the headmistress and the hippie."

"Oh, snap," Jac declared.

We settled back into our seats, and I felt a wave of contentment. I was with Jac, and I was traveling out of the country for the first time; we were going to visit museums and restaurants and historic sites all over Montreal. Why shouldn't we have fun? The new school year had barely started, and anything seemed possible. So what if our mothers needed to be kept away from each other and all of the Satellite Girls?

So what if Ben Greenblott was sitting three rows in back of me?

I guess I forgot to mention it. I liked a boy. That boy.

It was weird, because I had known Ben Greenblott, at least as a "hi" friend, for two years. We had been lab partners a couple of times in bio and always seemed to end up in most of the same classes. And for the first year and forty-nine weeks of that time, I'm sorry to say I barely noticed him at all. He just registered as regular and unremarkable in every conceivable way. Your basic nice guy whom everyone likes but who keeps a low profile.

Then out of the blue, about three weeks ago, just after school opened, I dropped my music in chorus, and Ben Greenblott picked it up for me. And as he handed it back, his regular brown eyes suddenly became hypnotic, velvety chocolate orbs. In about four seconds, the rest of him transformed from unmemorable to cupcake. I took in his jet-black hair, his caramel-colored skin, and his strong hands holding my copy of "Kumbaya." The place behind my kneecaps went all squeaky. And I've been thinking about him, like *constantly*, every single day since.

So yeah. School trip. Best friend. Mothers who must not come into close contact with each other. Satellite Girls.

And the love of my eighth-grade life, who had no idea that I worshipped and adored him on a daily basis, or that I saw dead people almost as often.

Somebody really ought to be writing all of this down.

Chapter 2

The border guard looked like he meant business. He stood at the front of the bus at the U.S.-Canada border stop, hands on hips. Behind him appeared a squirrelly-looking guy in a different uniform, with Coke-bottle glasses, tight thin lips, and a forehead that was way too big for his face. Mrs. Redd, who insisted on being addressed in French class as Madame Rouge, swept up the aisle to meet them.

"Purpose of the journey?" the border guard asked, sounding bored.

"Class trip to Montreal," Mrs. Redd declared. "These are all my students."

She gestured toward us proudly, as if there were any doubt where we might be lurking. She beamed at the border guard like we were a bus full of Rhodes Scholars and pageant queens. He looked unimpressed.

"Passports out," he said in a clipped tone.

"*Produisez les passports*," Mrs. Redd repeated to us loudly in completely unnecessary French.

The guard started with Jac's mom, whose passport was no doubt in perfect order with a professional, airbrushed photo. My mom had never had a passport before — could he tell this was her first? He took the document, glanced at her, and put it back in her hand. Then the border guard systematically worked his way down the aisle. Jac and I handed over our passports silently. As the border guard examined them, the squirrelly guy behind him narrowed his eyes at me.

The guard handed back our documents silently and moved on, but his friend with the massive forehead hung back for a moment. Our eyes locked. He gazed at me suspiciously. I had the sudden and acute sensation that he could be a real jerk.

"Bring nothing and no one back from Montreal," he said to me in a reedy voice, "or you will be in violation of federal law. If you attempt to bring anything or anyone back over the border, you will. Be. Prosecuted. To the fullest extent of the law. Understood?"

My mouth was hanging open. What was he picking on me for? Did I look like a smuggler? But I'd watched too many episodes of *Locked Up Abroad*, and I didn't want to be the first eighth grader in my school to end up in a Canadian prison. So I nodded very seriously.

For a minute I thought the squirrel guard was not satisfied with my earnest response. He stared at me for another minute, hands on hips.

"I'll be keeping an eye on you," he declared. Then he scuttled down the aisle to catch up with his boss.

When he seemed out of earshot, I turned to Jac.

"What did he single me out for?" I asked.

Jac gave me a blank look.

"Delusions of grandeur already?" she asked. "If you hadn't noticed, Kit Kat, he's looking at everybody's passport."

"Not him, the other guy...okay, never mind," I said quickly.

Jac's eyebrows shot up.

"Other guy?" she asked.

I began to untie and retie the shoelace on one of my sneakers. Jac leaned toward me.

"Is there a ghost on the bus?" she whispered eagerly.

If you see spirits wherever you go, it is probably just as well that you have a best friend who thinks this is a cool and exciting thing and does not think you are a pathological liar, a nut, or a gatekeeper to the realm of evil. But sometimes Jac's enthusiasm was a little irritating.

"Kat, spit it out!" she said, a little louder.

I shushed her, and looked around.

"There's a guy with thick glasses and a huge forehead who got on the bus with the border guard. He, like, warned me about bringing stuff back over the border from Canada. Stuff or people, actually. He said he'd be keeping an eye on me."

Eyes wide, Jac pressed her little hands to her chest. She looked utterly thrilled.

"Where is the ghost right now?" Jac whispered.

I sighed, then discreetly turned and looked behind me.

The squirrel guy was glaring up the aisle at me as the border guard took and examined a passport from....oh. My head snapped front again. Ben Greenblott.

"He's back there with B...that guy... Whatjamacallhim, Bob Graybean or whatever his name is."

"Whatjamacallhim? You know his name. Just Monday you were Googling it to see if Greenblott was Ukrainian because you said you might do an extra credit report on Ukrainian immigrants in our area. How can you have forgotten that already? You're not getting carsick, are you? You look funny. We're not even moving right now. Is it the bathroom smell? Because I don't like it, either."

Yeah. I know it's terrible. Jac was my best friend, and I usually told her everything. She knew my deepest secrets, about seeing dead people and helping Earthbound spirits cross over, like my mother did, all that. I had been party to every development in her "Should I be a cellist/should I quit the cello?" drama that had been unfolding since last year, when we met. But I had not yet told her that Ben Greenblott from bio class had recently been elevated in status, unbeknownst to him, from random guy to soul mate. And when she had caught me Googling his name, I made up the ridiculous Ukrainian story instead of telling her the truth.

I was afraid to tell her for several reasons. First of all, it was embarrassing. Second of all, if I told her, she would *know*. And then she'd be paying close attention to anything I said or did around Ben Greenblott — she'd want to discuss and dissect it later. That might make me act weird. Or, it could be humiliating, because it would inevitably lead to the con-clusion that Ben Greenblott did not care whether or not I existed.

Plus, right now nobody in the entire world knew that when I sat and stared out the win-dow or off into space or sometimes even when I was pretending to read, I was really lost in the imaginary world of Ben Greenblott. Or, more specifically, me and Ben Greenblott. So, though it was almost killing me to keep the identity of my soul mate a secret, I decided I would remain silent about it, at least for now. I could always change my mind later.

"Yep," I said. Then I turned and gave Jac a smile that probably looked weird.

"Yep what? You really are acting strange, Voodoo Mama. Know what I think?"

She leaned in close to me. Oh no. She prob-ably already knew. Jac knew me like nobody else in the world did. She could probably tell everything I was thinking about Ben, whether I confessed it or not. I needed to change the subject, because if Jac confronted me with the truth, I would have no choice but to fess up. Luckily, there was one other thing I hadn't yet told her. I knew it would make an excellent diversion.

"My mother had Orin over to dinner Saturday," I told her. "He's taking care of Max while we're away, and he came by to get the leash and his food bowls and chew toys and stuff."

Jac looked simultaneously dismayed and thrilled. I was under standing orders to include Jac in any activity in which my mom's über-hot un-boyfriend Orin might appear. She grabbed my arm, then peeked over the seats to make sure our mothers were still safe in their rows. She opened her mouth, then snapped it shut as the border guard and the squirrel strode up the aisle.

"All clear — bus driver, you're good to go," announced the guard.

Tim stood up and adjusted his uniform.

"Motor coach operator," he declared. The border guard either didn't hear or pretended not to. He got off the bus without another word. But Tim had defended his title, and you had to respect him for that.

Squirrel man paused at the front of the bus, turned toward me, and jabbed his index finger in my direction. Then he pointed two fingers in a V shape to his eyes and back at my eyes in the international "I'm watching you" gesture. So clichéd. Maybe he was from one of those old-time uncool decades. There was a hissing sound as the bus door closed and the engine roared to life. Jac had not released the death grip on my arm.

"Why didn't you call me? How was he?

What was he wearing? You like Orin, right? I mean, he's so good-looking, and he's a healer and helped you out with that demon thing at the Mountain House and the medium that was haunting your room — I still can't believe he knows all that stuff about fighting entities with energy...you like him, right? I like him. Your mom obviously likes him. Do you think they ever might actually date? I think they might. But it's cool with you? Did she dress up? Did you dress up? What did you eat?"

It could have been irritating. It could have, but it wasn't. Jac's barrage of questions hit me more like a fresh breeze than a gale-force wind. Odd as it sounds, it was way easier to talk about the cute guy in my mother's life than to admit there was a boy in mine, especially since they were just friends. And the fact that Jac was rarely able to talk about Orin without pointing out his gray-haired, shaggy handsomeness was also, at this moment, endearing rather than excruciating.

I glanced out the window. The road signs were now in French. I had just left the country for the first time in my life. We got to miss a whole Friday of classes. We had an adventure ahead of us. I turned and smiled at Jac's gleaming, eager face.

"Okay," I said. "So what happened was…"

And Jac settled happily into her seat to hear the tale of a routine dinner with Orin as the bus sped toward Montreal.

Outside, the sky had darkened, and it began to rain.

Chapter 3

We had only three days in Montreal, and Mrs. Redd was determined that not a second be wasted. So instead of going to our hotel to unload after the three-and-a-half-hour trip, we drove straight to our first official tourist destination: the Basilique Notre-Dame. I was tired and cranky and wanted nothing more than to unpack my suitcase and flop down on a hotel bed for a nap, but when our bus pulled up to the massive cathedral, my jaw dropped.

It towered above the city square where it

was built. Even with the miserable gray background of the storm clouds and drizzling rain, the whole stone structure stood out, as if it were glowing from within.

"It's gigantic," I whispered to Jac. "Have you ever seen anything like it?"

"Well, Notre Dame in Paris," she said. "And Montmartre. And of course Winchester Cathedral, and Westminster Abbey in London. St. Peter's Basilica in Rome, obviously. And, oh, what's that one on the thing by the place…?"

Oh. I had momentarily forgotten that Jac had traveled to cello competitions all over the world. I was probably the only one on the entire bus who had never been to Europe, let alone out of the country.

"Oh, but no, I mean yeah, it's just amazing!" Jac said quickly, with way too much enthusiasm. "No, it's more beautiful than any cathedral I've ever seen. Really, there's just something…about it!"

I smiled. I appreciated the gesture. Jac's father was some sort of computer guy who earned a good living, so the Grays had money, and we didn't. My father had left us four years ago with barely a few words since. There were things Jac had done and seen that I might never experience. Of course, that went both ways. Jac had never been yelled at by a dead person, nor had she been instrumental in guiding a confused and very deceased medium into the light, or chased by a black demonic cloud. The house next door to hers had never been haunted by a whole slew of spirits that wouldn't leave her alone, and restless ghosts didn't toss books around in the school library to get her attention. And still, despite all those differences, we were best friends. The middle-school medium and the cello genius.

"*Alors, mes enfants*," Mrs. Redd was saying. "*Écoutez.*"

Why did she insist on speaking to us in French? Mrs. Redd was a round dumpling of a woman, only about Jac's height, which is tiny. She was almost as wide as she was high, and she favored large men's shirts that came down to her knees and made her look like the Liberty Bell.

"*Nous attendons notre…notre…* all right, we're waiting for our guide, Sid, to join us, and then we will proceed, immediately, into this magnificent cathedral."

On cue, Tim the Motor Coach Operator pushed a button and the door hissed open. A young, dark-haired man in a leather jacket and a black-and-white checked scarf wrapped around his neck got onto the bus. He was so different from what I'd expected — I thought tour guides were always frumpy middle-aged women — that I assumed for a minute that he was dead.

"He's adorable," whispered Jac.

Not dead, then.

There was a PA system on the bus, which the guide turned on.

"Hey, guys," he said, in a slightly accented voice. "I'm Sid. *Je m'appelle Sid. Qui parles français?*"

Judging by the shouted responses of "Moi," a great many more people, especially girls, could miraculously respond to a French question when it was spoken by Sid rather than Mrs. Redd.

"It's okay, though, we can talk in English, too. I know you are tired, but we're gonna go into this amazing cathedral right now, la Basilique Notre-Dame, and it's gonna blow your minds. It's better than French rap music even, so get ready."

Mrs. Redd looked a little suspicious, like maybe even a Canadian shouldn't mention French rap and the Basilique Notre-Dame in the same sentence, but a great cheer had begun in the back of the bus. Sid had navigated the sixty-second window of opportunity eighth graders generally give an adult before they are judged "cool" or "uncool," and the verdict was clear. Sid was cool.

We filed off the bus. My mom stood off to one side staring up at the cathedral. She must have felt my eyes on her, because she turned and gave me a quick wink. Jac's mother was standing about four feet away, fiddling with an iPhone, not even noticing the cathedral. She looked even more severe than usual. I smiled at my mother and wondered how she was going to survive three days with Jac's mom. Actually, I wondered how *I* was going to survive it.

From the sidewalk, I could now see the

cathedral in its entirety. It loomed up like a castle, complete with two huge rectangular towers at each end. There were three massive arched wooden doors in front with larger stone arches over them, and three more between the two square towers, each housing a statue. Staring up at the old stone and stained glass, I felt I had tumbled through the centuries, back hundreds of years.

"Nice," Jac said.

Nice.

"Okay, guys, so we're gonna walk in," Sid was saying.

"We're going to walk in," Mrs. Redd repeated, like she was translating for us. Except that Sid was, you know, speaking English already.

"Okay, so this is a very famous church," Sid called over his shoulder, as we trotted on the walkway behind him like ducklings.

"Very famous," Mrs. Redd echoed. "To put it in perspective for you all, none other than *Celine Dion* was married here!"

"What, that chick who sings the *Titanic* theme song?" called the shortest and squattest of the random jock boys. "Outstanding!"

It was starting to rain as we gathered by the central wooden door. It looked as if it had been built for giants. I felt a surge of excitement and happiness.

"Hey, Spooky, is your mom even allowed to go in there?" I heard.

I turned to see Brooklyn Bigelow, rocking her newest razor-cut trendy hair, which was colored and highlighted within an inch of its life. I stayed away from Brooklyn whenever possible, but I'd had enough encounters with her to know she had an exaggerated contempt for all things supernatural, which she declared to be "against religion," though she did not seem to have any functioning knowledge of what religion was.

She thought my mother, who made no attempt to hide the fact that she communicated with the dead for a living, might as well have a little pair of devil horns sticking up through her hair. I also knew Brooklyn's supposed disgust concealed a very real terror of all things ghostly. It was knowledge I tried not to take advantage of, though at times like this it was very, very difficult.

"You have something in your teeth," I said, before turning away.

"Ew — you do," Jac echoed at her, squeezing my arm.

Brooklyn was always suspicious of anything I said to her, but her vanity was more powerful, and she ducked her head and began fishing in her gargantuan purse for a pocket mirror.

"She thinks she's some kind of genius for coming up with the name Spooky," I said, flushing with irritation.

"She stole it from *The X-Files*. I hate her," Jac declared.

And just like that my irritation dissolved. Sometime it's enough for your best friend to state she hates the same person you do. It's just enough.

We walked through the big wooden door through a small, screened ticket area. When our line moved beyond the screen, I stopped in my tracks and gasped.

It was so huge. It was so ethereal. It was so *beautiful*.

Enormous wooden columns lined each side of the church, a delicious mix of wood and paint and gilt. The air smelled like incense and candles and furniture polish. The ceiling, impossibly high, was a rich blue and covered with golden stars. At the far end behind the altar stood something I hardly knew how to describe—a building-sized golden framework of arched windows and towers housing life-sized painted statues of various figures, prophets, or saints, I guessed. Behind the framework the wall had been painted to look like a deep blue sky dotted with clouds.

I was speechless.

I looked around to see how everyone else was taking it.

Sid was standing in the center aisle counting us, Mrs. Redd at his side imitating his counting. Beside her stood Mrs. Gray, who looked like she was trying in vain to get a signal on her iPhone. My mom was sitting in one of the pews, her eyes closed.

The other students were standing stock still at various places in the center aisle staring, open-mouthed, grabbing each other and pointing at things. A few had started taking pictures. I was almost gratified to see that even Brooklyn Bigelow looked stunned by the magnificence of the architecture around her. So she was human after all. A little, anyway.

And Ben Greenblott. He had walked over to one of the huge carved wooden pillars, and as I watched he reached out very gently and brushed the wood with his fingertips. Then he closed his eyes, like he was absorbing the feel of the wood. For a moment, he looked as beautiful and ethereal as any of the statues in this church.

Yep — it was definitely love.

Ben had apparently caught Brooklyn's attention, too. She had arranged herself in one of her *Entertainment Tonight* poses — one hand on her hip, the other twisting a lock of her hair through several well-manicured fingers. She shot Ben a look through lowered eyelids, but he seemed totally unaware of her. I wanted to hurl a prayer book at her silly flirting head. Didn't she know Ben Green-blott was way too good for her?

Sid was talking now — his voice went in and out of my consciousness as I tried to recover from the daze I felt.

"...building completed in 1829...gothic style...hand painted..."

But another voice was intruding.

"...la...C'est mal, la fenêtre...elle est trop claire...trop chaude...elle ne marche pas, la fenêtre..."

I felt dizzy. I couldn't tell where the voice was coming from. I wasn't sure what it was saying, though I knew from our most recent vocab quiz that *fenêtre* meant window. And *mal* meant bad. The window was bad? How could a window be bad?

"...Okay, guys, so we're gonna go into the

little chapel in the back now, so you can see how they rebuilt it after the fire...," Sid was saying.

"Kat, are you coming?"

Jac was standing right next to me, peering into my face a little anxiously. It was only then that I realized I had totally spaced out for some time. Our group had followed Sid almost to the very front of the church. Brooklyn had abandoned her "look at me" pose and followed. Only Jac and I were still standing in the aisle.

And one other person.

Ben Greenblott was still standing by the wooden pillar I'd seen him touching.

"We'll get in trouble if they realize we're not with them," Jac said. "Come on!"

She began marching up the aisle, shooting looks over her shoulder to make sure I was following her.

"I, um... think we're supposed to go now," I said, awkwardly directing my voice in Ben's direction. He looked at me. I looked... away.

"Wow, yeah," Ben said. "I kind of zoned out. Thanks, Kat."

He was so nice.

We began to walk up the aisle — our group had disappeared around the back of the altar in the direction of the little chapel. *Think of something to say, you nitwit*, I silently screamed at myself.

"It's hard to picture it was ever there, isn't it?" Ben asked.

He had spoken again. To me. We. Were. Talking.

"Yeah. I mean, what? Picture..."

Oh. Prizewinning banter, Kat, great job.

"The window," he said.

Wait. What?

"The window?" I asked.

I did not see any windows anywhere in the direction Ben was pointing, which was by the altar and the golden towered thing with the statues, a painted blue sky peeking out from behind.

"Sid said there used to be a huge stained glass window there," Ben replied. "And the sun would come directly in during mass and everyone complained it was too bright and too hot. So they eventually plastered the window over and built that."

The window was bad. *Trop claire, trop chaude.* Too light, too hot. But who had been telling me this?

People get information from the dead in all different kinds of ways. Both my mom and I are what you call clairvoyant—we see ghosts. We can interact with them and talk to them and stuff, but the main connection at first is usually visual. But some mediums do it differently — and the ones who hear voices are called clairaudient. I wasn't supposed to be one of those.

In the seven months since I'd turned thirteen and seen my first spirit, it had taken all that I had to start getting used to the fact that I saw dead people. One way or another, I knew I was going to be able to deal with it.

Unless I started hearing voices, too.

Chapter 4

When we were all back in our seats on the bus, Sid and Mrs. Redd began another of what I was sure would be hundreds of head counts. I thought life might be considerably improved if we returned to the U.S. with a couple fewer Satellite Girls than we'd come with, but I wasn't making policy. Sid counted in English, and Mrs. Redd translated his counting into French, like we were at the United Nations or something.

"*Seven, eight, nine…*" Sid pointed to each person as he counted.

"*Sept, huit, neuf...*" Mrs. Redd echoed. She didn't point, because I guess there was no way to accurately do that in French.

Jac had sloshed some of her Sprite onto the floor and was bent over double mopping it up. I tucked my feet under me so my sneakers wouldn't get sticky, and out of sheer boredom began silently counting along with Sid. When he got to seventeen, he gave a satisfied nod and stopped counting.

Except I got to eighteen.

I guess I counted someone twice.

Jac was still in cleanup mode, so I counted again. And came up with the same result. Four adults including Sid, and eighteen students.

But there were only seventeen of us on the trip. There had been only seventeen of us in the cathedral, and seventeen in the gift shop behind the little chapel.

I leaned into the aisle and examined each row as nonchalantly as I could. We had pretty much taken the same seats we'd had for the trip up. In the back, I could see Shoshanna and Brooklyn, orbited by other girlcraft I recognized only too well, totaling one planet (Shoshanna) and six Satellite Girls.

Directly in front of the girls were four Random Boys, two of them super jocks and loud, one of them a sporty hanger-on type, and a techno guy named Phil who had successfully morphed his image this year from geek-freak to geek-chic. When someone's iPod or cell phone got messed up, Phil became even more popular.

Lumped together on the other side of the bus were the only four kids not in our French class: They were from the Foreign Students Club and had therefore been eligible to join the trip. I knew and liked the quiet, sweet-faced Mikuru Miyazaki, an exchange student from Japan, who sat with her lethally over-protective brother, Yoshi. Next to them was the terminally silent Alice Flox, and directly across the aisle was the bubbly and outgoing Indira Desai.

Then, of course, there was the seat I was most trying to pretend I wasn't looking at, in which sat Ben Greenblott. Across the row from him, in the window seat with her face pressed to the glass was...was...

Who was that?

She was nondescript from the back. Her hair was shoulder length, sandy colored, and straight. She wore a beige sweater that my mom could have worn like fifty years ago, and khaki-colored pants.

Maybe she'd gotten separated from her own group and had accidentally gotten on our bus.

I decided to do a good deed.

"Back in a sec," I told Jac, who responded with a "Mmph" while she continued to do damage control on her soda spill.

I got up, stretched, then moved into the empty row of seats in front of Beige Girl. I stuck my face into the gap between the window seat and the window. I could see her profile, but her face was masked by a hand pressed against the glass.

"Hey," I said quietly. "How's it going?"

I thought she might have moved a little, almost like a flinch of surprise, but she made no indication she'd heard me.

"Hey," I said again. "You're not from our school, are you?"

Nothing.

I put my hands on the back of the seat, rose on my knees, and peered directly down at her.

"Hey," I repeated, much louder.

This time she looked at me, dropping her hand away from the glass.

She was very delicate looking, with porcelain skin and huge, pale blue eyes. There was a buzz of energy around her.

She was, to put it bluntly, very dead.

When, when, when was I going to stop confusing the living with the dead? It was so totally uncool.

"I can see you," I said very quietly. I could not remember the French word for *see*. "*Je...* um...*see-ez vous.*"

She looked at me with mild interest and no readable expression, then turned back to the window, obscuring her face from mine.

I was getting ready to ask her if she needed help, or maybe find an extremely tactful English-French phrase for "Do you know that you're dead?" when I happened to glance across the aisle.

Ben Greenblott was looking at me.

Ben Greenblott, more accurately, was watching me have a conversation with an empty seat.

There are no words to describe the mortification I felt.

Without saying goodbye or even sneaking another look at Beige Girl, I faced forward and slumped down in the seat. I closed my eyes, trying to make myself disappear. Then I felt rather than saw someone standing over me. Living? Dead? I kept my eyes squeezed shut. All the possibilities seemed equally agonizing at this moment.

"Kat? Are you okay?"

I opened my eyes.

"Mom."

I felt an initial tide of relief sweep over me. She probably realized something embarrassing had just happened to me. My mom could almost always fix things. If not fix them, improve them a great deal. I almost patted the seat beside me, ready to whisper secrets about Ben Greenblott and how Brooklyn called me Spooky and the disembodied French voice in the Basilique Notre-Dame.

Then I saw my mother glance very quickly at the seat behind me.

She was a medium. Naturally, she saw Beige Girl, too. And suddenly I was overwhelmed with frustration. She had come back here to check out the ghost, not probe my feelings on the subject of the perfect boy.

Was it not enough that I had the gift of second sight dumped on me without any say in the matter whatsoever? Was it not enough that there were times a virtual village of dead people followed me around, trying to get my attention? Was it not enough that if there was a demon within a five-mile radius, it would sense my presence and come at me?

I just wanted to be normal. Not forever. Just, say, for the Montreal trip. Just while Ben Greenblott was sitting a few feet away. Just for the moment. I did not want to talk about ghosts.

"I'm fine," I mumbled.

"Are you sure?" she pressed. She tucked a strand of baby-fine blond hair behind one ear and stared at me, her forehead creased. I have my father's coloring—jet-black hair and green eyes. For a split second, my mother looked like a complete stranger.

"I just need some space," I said. I could have said it more nicely. But Ben Greenblott was sitting right there. I had been talking to air. He had seen it.

It was not okay.

My mother nodded, like she understood about the ghost situation without my having to say anything. Which made me even more irritated with her. She could sense a spirit a mile off, but she couldn't sense that I had just humiliated myself in front of the only boy I wanted to impress. Wouldn't a regular mother have noticed that?

"I'm going to go sit down, then," she said.

Part of me wanted to call after her. She was going to sit by herself, and Jac's mom wasn't going to talk to her, and I loved her and didn't want her to be alone.

But I didn't. I stayed where I was. When the bus's engine started up, I ducked my head, got up, and slipped back into the seat next to Jac.

"Where'd you go? Did you try the bathroom? Was it terrible?"

I said nothing, just shot her a smile.

It was definitely not okay.

Chapter 5

"I cannot eat this," Brooklyn Bigelow was declaring loudly. "I cannot eat anything on this menu."

The waitress stared at Brooklyn with mild amusement. She was young and chic, with wild thick black hair and perfectly applied bloodred lipstick. She wore a black T-shirt, skinny jeans that clung to her as if their life depended on it, and shiny black gladiator boots laced all the way up to her knee. She looked like she had tumbled out of the latest edition of *Vogue Paris*.

"Do you have a salad?" Brooklyn asked, very slowly and loudly. Brooklyn appeared to think that raising the volume of her English would make it more understandable to those who spoke other languages.

"Sahh-ladd?" Brooklyn repeated.

"Brook, it's a poutine restaurant," Shoshanna said. The Satellite Girls had commandeered one end of the long table. "That's what they have. That's all they serve. Poutine. Get over it."

Frankly, I had assumed Sid was having a bit of a joke on us when he described the fare available at our first official meal. Poutine was essentially a plate of french fries covered in gravy and liberally doused with chunks of something he called squeaky cheese. We had arrived at the restaurant with voracious appetites—even Jac's stick-thin mother was casting anxious looks in the direction of the kitchen. The adults had their own table, and the rest of us were sitting at one long table clutching menus.

I was at the end opposite the Satellite Girls, with Jac to my right. Directly across from me was Ben Greenblott. I had so far pretended, I think very convincingly, not to have noticed he was there. Instead I focused on the unfolding drama around Brooklyn.

"Havez-vous le steamed vegetables?" Brooklyn asked. "Knowez-vous les foods on le Zone Diet? Le South Beach?"

"Brook, zip it," Shoshanna said, not bothering to conceal her irritation. She twisted a lock of shiny dark hair between her fingers, opened her phone and snapped it shut again, then physically turned her back on her number one Satellite Girl and began talking to number two, Lacy Fowler, instead.

"Havez-vous le grapefruit?" Brooklyn pressed.

Jac snickered.

"Havez-vous," she muttered. "Does she actually think that's French?"

The waitress took the menu from Brooklyn and pointed at it, the way you'd show a kid in kindergarten an illustration from a picture book.

"We don't *havez* anything but poutine," she said in perfect unaccented English. "You can have fries plain, with meat, Italian style, Mexican style, or extra cheesy. What's it gonna be?"

"Brooklyn, come on," shouted one of the sporty boys. "We're starving here. Just pick one."

"Just pick one," chimed in other voices, most of them male.

Alice leaned over and whispered something to Indira, who began giggling wildly. On Alice's other side, Mikuru gazed down at her plate and smiled. It wasn't often one of the Satellite Girls made a scene.

Shoshanna turned and gave her devoted slave a pointed, unpleasant look.

"Pick one," she commanded.

Brooklyn instantly pointed at something on the menu, pressed her thin lips together, and made a sour face.

"Small, large, or extra large?" the waitress asked.

"Small," Brooklyn whispered. "And a Diet Coke." A cheer erupted from the Random Sport Guys.

"There better be a Stairmaster at this hotel," Brooklyn muttered.

Once the obstacle of Brooklyn had been overcome, the waitress made swift progress taking orders around the table, ignoring the worshipful glances the guys threw her way.

"This is so great," Jac said. "We're, like, getting school credit for eating. I wonder if they have cake here?"

Jac had inherited her mother's tiny frame, though I knew from close personal observation that she ate more than any human being I had ever encountered and was especially partial to food groups in the chocolate family.

"We check into the hotel after this, right?" I asked.

"I think so," Jac replied. "Ben — do you have a copy of the schedule on you?"

What? Why was Jac talking to Ben? Because I hadn't told her not to, I thought. I hadn't told her that the plan was to pretend Ben didn't exist, because he had seen me talking to an invisible friend.

"Yep," he said. He reached into the pocket of his jeans, pulled out a folded piece of paper, and scanned it. I snuck a look at his large brown eyes while he read, then held on to the table while the room lurched a bit.

"After dinner we check in at the hotel and have unpacking and free time; nine o'clock we have to be in our rooms for the night; and ten lights out."

"And tomorrow? Kat, are you listening?"

Why wouldn't I be listening? How did my best friend in the world suddenly develop a thick sponge of mush between her ears?

I nodded. Ben hadn't taken his eyes off the schedule.

"I'm listening," I said, so quietly I barely heard myself say it.

"Tomorrow is pajama breakfast, then Mont-Royal and surrounding sights, and in the afternoon the Biodome."

"Which one are you looking forward to most, Kat?" Jac asked.

Why had Jac chosen this time and place to become Oprah? Her perky questions and conversation-making were beginning to freak me out. I was saved by the arrival of the bombshell waitress.

"Mexican poutine, large, please," Jac declared. "And a Coke."

"Italian small poutine, please," I said. "And a root beer."

I examined the waitress's gladiator boots as she directed her attention at my soul mate. And suddenly couldn't stand her.

"Regular medium, *s'il vous plaît*," Ben said. "*Et aussi un* root beer."

"*Bon, merci*," said the bombshell, and floated away, presumably powered by the sheer force of her good looks.

I was getting ready to ponder whether Ben

ordering the same soda as me was a) coincidence; b) a secret message; or c) subtle mockery, when a man in a black suit approached our table and stood directly behind Ben, scowling. He had the thickest, darkest eyebrows I had ever seen, and they were pushed together to emphasize his expression. He leaned forward, half through and half around Ben, and spoke directly to me, pounding his fist on the table to emphasize each word.

"*Je n'aime pas le poutine,*" he declared emphatically.

Fool me once, shame on you and all that — but I wasn't going to make the mistake again of thinking this guy was among the living. I was sure there was no visible reaction on my face to his declaration that he did not like poutine. The guy whumped the table with his hand one more time, then stood up straight and took a step back. I gave him a look that said, "Back up off me, bro."

And Ben Greenblott turned in his seat and for the briefest of moments directed his gaze to the precise spot where the man was. When the poutine-hater abruptly turned on his heel and stalked away, Ben turned back at the table and gave me a strange look.

Apparently I was not as clever as I thought. Ben had seen me react to the man after all. Correction—he had seen me react to someone who for all practical purposes was not there.

"I need to find the restroom," I mumbled, standing up clumsily. Before Jac could offer to go with me, which she usually did, I walked away. Fortunately the little shape-in-a-dress symbol that means ladies' room in America looks the same in Montreal, so I located it easily. As I walked across the restaurant, I noticed that the man in the dark suit was visiting every table in the room to declare his disdain for the only dish on the menu. Nobody seemed to see him. Big surprise.

I paused by the bathroom door and shot a look over to the adults' table. My mother was watching the phantom poutine hater with a small smile on her lips. As usual she seemed to feel me looking at her. She met my gaze, widened her smile, then nodded toward the poutine hater and gave a small "Whatcha gonna do with these crazy ghosts?" shrug. I felt unaccountably mad at her, and turned away without acknowledging her. As I walked through the bathroom door, I felt a rush of guilt and a bad heat rising in my stomach.

I had pretended not to see my mother.

Not okay.

Chapter 6

"Is that all? Kat, I thought it was something really serious. I thought you were dying or expelled or maybe you'd made friends with Brooklyn."

I gave my friend an amused look. She was lying on one of the two double beds, munching on a Twix bar between slurps of some sort of Canadian canned chocolate drink. Our hotcl room was small, the TV worked, there was free stuff in the bathroom, and it all seemed blessedly unhaunted. Good times.

"Isn't it enough? Jac, in one breath I just confessed to liking a boy and being mad at my mom for no reason. Throw me a bone here."

Instead, she threw me a piece of her Twix, which I bit into.

"Okay, well, let's start with Ben Green-blott. I think he's perfect for you. I actually thought so even before you told me you liked him. Didn't you notice how I was trying to get a conversation started at dinner?"

"I noticed," I said, ruefully. "I was trying to pretend he wasn't there."

"You shouldn't do that," Jac said. "He'll think you don't like him. He's a nice guy — you should talk to him. And it's not like he's hanging out with anyone else on this trip."

It was true. Ben was friendly to everyone, but he didn't seem to be friends *with* anyone in particular. He was hard to categorize.

Though I knew he was a straight honor roll kid, he was not clearly a geek, a brain, or another brand of outcast. People seemed to like him well enough. But he kept a low profile at school, and kind of kept to himself.

"Okay, but what about the part where he saw me talking to an empty seat?"

"Saw you talking to *yourself*," Jac corrected. "Plenty of people do that. Einstein talked to himself—and so does Shoshanna Longbarrow."

Wow. It was a sure bet this was the first time in recorded history Shoshanna Longbarrow had ever been mentioned in the same sentence with Einstein.

"It still isn't good," I said.

"It isn't a reason to write him off either," Jac insisted. "And you need a little encouragement sometimes. Did you ever e-mail that guy from the Mountain House?" she asked.

Jac enjoyed bugging me about the not-so-cute boy I'd met at the massive old hotel we'd been to that spring.

"Just the one time," I said. "Jac, I wasn't exactly chomping at the bit to become Mrs. Ted Kenyon. The guy's going to end up working at the most haunted mountain resort ever."

"He liked you," Jac said, licking the inside of the Twix wrapper fastidiously. "That's allz I'm saying."

"That doesn't mean Ben Greenblott likes me," I declared.

"It doesn't mean he *doesn't* like you," Jac countered. She reached below the bed and produced a Mars Bar. I couldn't help but laugh.

"What? They're like Milky Ways but better. Everybody says so."

There was a knock on the door. Jac shoved

the Mars Bar under a pillow, so she obviously felt it was her mother stopping by.

I got up and opened the door, confirming Jac's unspoken suspicion.

"Oh, Kat," Mrs. Gray said, sounding surprised to see me, like she didn't realize I was along on the trip. "I need a word with Jacqueline."

"I'm right here," Jac said, sitting up, but she made no move to stand. Jac was usually either openly at war with her mother or in an uneasy truce. This qualified as an uneasy truce.

"This ee-phone…"

"iPhone," Jac corrected. "Like I Spy."

Mrs. Gray took a not-quite-patient breath and held the offending piece of technology out.

"This eye-phone is not working," she said. "I was told it was the very best, and it doesn't seem to work at all. I can't make a simple phone call."

"Well, did you call to enable international dialing?" Jac asked.

Mrs. Gray looked mystified.

"It was on the trip memo," Jac said. "Here — if you need to make a call, just use my phone for now. And if you want your iPhone figured out, talk to that kid Phil. He figures out everybody's phones."

She tossed her phone at her mother, who not only didn't catch it but barely managed to be hit in the head by it. I retrieved the phone off the floor and handed it to Mrs. Gray.

"Thank you," she said, to one or both of us. "Oh, and we're meant to announce that there is a quick meeting everyone has to attend at eight forty-five by the soda machines."

She left, closing the door quietly behind her.

"Jac," I said. "You shouldn't throw things at your mother. You could have put her eye out."

Jac shrugged.

I opened my mouth to suggest that Jac consider being a teensy bit nicer to her mother but remembered how angry the same suggestion had made Jac during our trip to the Mountain House. So, I decided to file away my comment for later.

"I'm going to brush my hair before the meeting," I said, walking into the bathroom.

"Here," Jac said, appearing suddenly behind me with her flowered cosmetics bag. "Have a squirt of this."

She spritzed me with something delicious smelling, a mix of orange blossoms and cloves. Jac obviously really was pro-Ben. I felt a little zap of nervousness in my toes. She pointed at my head.

"Dangly earrings," she commanded.

"Really? The crescent moon ones? You don't think they're too much?"

"I think they're perfect," she said. "They're very you."

I found the earrings in question and put them on. I went into the bathroom and stared at myself in the mirror.

Sometimes I looked so much like my father it made me furious. I didn't like being reminded of him. But there he was in the mirror. I had his good hair—thick and dark and glossy—and I wore mine long. I had his odd sea-green eyes, but my pale skin and the shape of my face, nose, and mouth were my mother's. Oh, and the whole "I see dead people" thing. That was all from mom's side of the family, too.

"We should probably go," Jac said. "I hear people out there."

I took a breath and gave myself a final once-over in the mirror. It wasn't bad. I had grown two inches over the summer, and my hair was getting to a decent length. I might not have a tiny waist and long, lean legs, like Shoshanna, but I was blessedly zit-free, and as un-teenage as it might be, I secretly felt a certain sense of satisfaction with the way that I looked, in spite of my flaws.

"Okay," I said. "I'm ready."

Our group was gathering, as advertised, in the alcove by the soda machines. Three of the Random Boys were tossing around a miniature football made of something squishy. Phil was attempting to engage Mikuru in conversation but was being practically body-checked by her brother, Yoshi.

Indira was chattering happily to Alice, who was examining the contents of the soda machine with great concentration. Shoshanna was sitting cross-legged on the floor holding a Montreal guidebook, Lacy on one side of her and Brooklyn on the other, both in identical poses. The other two Satellite Girls, Shelby and Stacy, were nowhere to be seen.

Perched on a wide windowsill with his legs propped up was Ben Greenblott, looking lost in a book. I quickly looked away, then took another peek. He totally hadn't noticed me. I adjusted my earrings, fiddled with my watch, and shifted my weight from one leg to the other. Then I took another tiny peek. This time Ben was looking at me.

Oh my.

Mrs. Redd appeared suddenly, a wide smile on her face. I quickly gave her my full attention. She was wearing a brightly colored sweatshirt that proclaimed J'AIME MONTRÉAL! in pink letters. Something very bad seemed to have happened to her gray, usually straight hair. It looked as though she had styled it with a table saw and a pitchfork.

"Now, where is…ah, there you are," Mrs. Redd said. I looked down the hall and saw Sid rapidly approaching, clipboard in one hand and walkie-talkie in the other. The missing Satellite Girls were meekly walking in front of him, looking slightly abashed.

"Okay, guys, so in case it wasn't clear, which I'm guessing it wasn't," Sid said, shooting Shelby and Stacy a look, "the lobby is off-limits without an adult, as is the gift shop, swimming pool, *bureau de change*, workout room, escalator, and any other location you can think of that is not your assigned room or this hallway. Got that, guys?"

"We got it, Sid," called Phil. This apparently sounded good, because it was immediately followed by a chorus of "We got it, Sid" from the masses.

I peeked at Ben. Nothing. Mrs. Redd was looking very hard at Shelby and Stacy like she was trying to decide whether or not to further pursue where Sid had found them. I didn't think she needed to worry. For all his casual coolness, I had a feeling nothing and no one was going to get past Sid on this trip. We probably didn't even need the other chaperones.

Which reminded me: Where was my mother? Where, for that matter, was Jac's mother?

"What happened to her hair?" Jac whispered, looking toward Mrs. Redd.

I shrugged. It took every ounce of strength I had not to sneak another look in Ben's direction.

"It's crowded. I think there's more room over there," Jac said, pointing in the direction of the windowsill where Ben Greenblott was, in my opinion, magnificently perched.

I smacked her hand down.

"Don't point! Are you nuts?" I hissed.

"We should go over there."

I turned toward her and grabbed her two tiny shoulders.

"Jac, please. Just leave it for now, okay? Please?"

Jac gave me a long look. Mrs. Redd was making a speech about the pajama breakfast. She sounded like a large fly buzzing to and fro in the background.

"Please?" I whispered again.

Jac sighed.

"Well," she said after a moment, "I guess there is something to be said for remaining at a distance. He can get the full picture that way."

I was glad Jac had dropped it, though truth be told the "full picture" was the last thing I wanted Ben Greenblott, or anyone else, to have of me.

Chapter 7

We got under way relatively early the next morning and had arrived at our first destination. Mrs. Redd was calling to us loudly to remember where we parked. Given that we had come on an enormous bus with a massive green leprechaun painted on the side, I didn't feel her concern was necessary. What did concern me was that the Beige Girl was still on the bus when we boarded it that morning.

She sat in the same seat she'd been in when I first saw her. She continued to stare out the window, and this time I did not attempt to engage her in conversation. When we all disembarked at the Mount-Royal Park guest area, Beige Girl made no move to leave.

Sid was directing us to follow him on the wide, paved path that led up Mont-Royal to the famous overlook at the Chalet du Mont-Royal. He was walking backward up the hill, talking to us as he moved. I was enjoying that Sid seemed to start every sentence with the same two words.

"Okay, guys, so I'm sure you've all done your homework, and you know that this place was visited and named in the 1500s by a famous French explorer named...Come on, guys, who knows this?"

"Jacques Cousteau," shouted Phil.

Sid rolled his eyes a little.

"Okay, guys, think it through, come on," Sid said.

"Jacques Cartier," offered Mikuru.

Sid clapped. "Excellent," he said. "And he called it Royal Mountain, *Mont-Royal*, and what do you think got its name from that?"

"Oh yeah, Montreal. That's, like, amazing!" exclaimed Shelby.

Was it? It didn't seem especially amazing to me.

"If you pick up the pace a little we can catch up to Ben," Jac said.

I opened my mouth to tell her to give it a rest, but closed it again. She was right. He wasn't that far ahead of us, walking by himself. Mont Royal Park was beautiful even on a day like this, which was bleak and gray as the day before but without the rain. The path was wide and easy, and the way up wasn't steep at all.

I glanced behind me, to see my mother and Mrs. Gray taking up the rear. My mother was wearing sensible if raggedy sneakers, but Jac's mom was wearing some kind of espadrille without socks. *She's going to get terrible blisters*, I thought. I looked away before either of them could notice I was checking them out.

"Maybe you're right," I told Jac, feeling as brave and terrified as a pilgrim embarking on a voyage to the New World. "We could...oh."

Ben had been alone a minute ago. But now there was a guy walking next to him, talking and gesturing with his hands.

"Forget it. That other guy is talking to him now," I said.

Jac grabbed my elbow.

"What other guy?" she whispered.

Oh no. Not again.

"Please tell me you're joking," I said to her, almost tripping on a little rock in the road.

Jac shook her head. "I don't see anyone with Ben," she told me. "You do?"

I sighed.

"I do," I repeated.

The guy had looked normal at first glance, but on closer examination I could see he was wearing britches — like the boys had worn in our Drama Club production of *Our Town* — not the long baggy shorts I'd taken them for. His shirt was made of a thick material and looked worn and patched. He was built like a football player, tall and solid and strong. Jac suddenly sped up and walked closer to them. To him. To whatever. What was she doing?

Anything was better than walking alone, so I caught up with her. I could hear the spirit with Ben now.

"*Où est Hochelaga? Hochelaga?*"

I could not understand him. The back of

his neck was a little dirty and sunburned over the muscles. Was he asking where Hochelaga was? Or who Hochelaga was? *Où* means "who," right?

"*Hochelaga!*" the ghost boy repeated with more urgency. He raised one hand, like he was going to whack Ben on the head. With arms like that, I'm betting he could have Ben airborne with a single blow. If he'd been, you know, from our physical reality and all that.

"Hey!" I exclaimed.

Ben stopped walking and turned around. I hadn't realized how close on his heels I was — I almost collided with him.

"Hey," he said.

"Hey," I said.

But of course, I had already said that.

"Hey," Jac said. She came up on my right elbow, so that she didn't stand between Ben and me.

"Hey," Ben said, a smile spreading over his face.

This was either the best or the worst thing that had happened to me in a long time. I was walking with Ben, which gave me an excuse to chat with him and be with him and just basically absorb his Ben-ness. Except that a big dead guy in britches with no shoes and unkempt blond hair was in the way, repeating things in a language I did not speak especially well. Wonderful. My first shot at making a good impression on Ben and something had already, well, come between us.

"I'm trying to picture what this must have looked like to Cartier four hundred years ago," Ben said. The ghost guy practically jumped in the air.

"*Cartier! Je dois revenir à l'Emerille avec Cartier, à Hochelaga.*"

Okay, I didn't get any of that except

Cartier and hosh-uh-laka. There was no way for me to communicate this to the ghost without talking out loud, which Ben would naturally assume was me talking to him. But I was going to have a very hard time talking to Ben if this ghost couldn't take a hint and shove off for a while. What could I say to both of them?

"Nope," was what I came up with.

"But he was here," said Ben.

"Hochelaga," said Britches.

"Was he right here?" I asked. Oh, please.

"I guess nobody really knows," Ben says. "There must be archeological evidence, though. They must have found some trace of him after all this time. Maybe there wasn't a camp, though. They would have stayed on their ship."

"*Aidez-moi. Répondez! C'est loin, Hochelaga?*"

Maybe Britches was mistaking Ben for this guy Hochelaga, which could be a problem. Ghosts could be very stubborn. The no-longer-living medium I had encountered at the Mountain House, Madame Serena, had persisted in believing for some time that she was alive and I was the ghost. Madame Serena had glommed onto me like icing on a Hostess Cup Cake. All I needed was for Britches to attach himself permanently to Ben. I would have a snowball's chance in the desert of ever having a regular conversation with him then.

"You should ask Sid. Both of you should," Jac said.

I couldn't process comments like "both of you" right now. I was losing track of who could see whom.

We walked in silence for a moment. I shot Jac a desperate look. She looked at what to her must be the empty space between Ben and me and raised her eyebrows. I nodded a little.

She understood the problem, but what could she possibly do about it?

"Okay, guys, so we're gonna come up to the overlook," Sid was calling. I tried to get Britches's attention.

"Ask that guy," I muttered to Britches, gesturing toward Sid with my head.

"Ask Sid about Cartier?" Ben asked.

Rats. He'd heard me.

"Oh, no. Well, if you want," I corrected. "I mean..."

I made a sudden decision that the current situation could not be salvaged.

"I better check on my...mother," I said.

"Oh. Okay," said Ben.

"Why?" asked Jac.

"*Hochelaga*!" insisted Britches.

I turned abruptly and headed for the rear of the group. My mother and Mrs. Gray were walking together, though they didn't seem to be talking at all.

My mother's face broke into a smile when she saw me. She hadn't expressed any anger about me ignoring her, nor did she now look surprised that I was talking to her.

"Hey, Kat," she said. "You okay? Need a Band-Aid?"

She was giving me an opportunity to stop at the side of the path with her. I'm sure she was perfectly aware of the fact that a ghost was up there with Jac and Ben. She'd been figuring out what the dead wanted for so long, I had no doubt she could understand what Britches wanted and have him dispatched in minutes.

But Britches had attached himself to Ben, and I didn't want my mother going and doing her stuff where Ben could see or hear it.

The irritation I felt at my mother the night before resurfaced. If she had been born normal, after all, then I might have been born the same way. Was that so much to ask — that a person's mother be born normal?

"A Chap Stick — I just need a Chap Stick," I muttered.

She fished around in her big, faded bag and produced one. Cherry flavored. Not my favorite.

"I know you don't like the cherry stuff, but it's all they had," she said, giving me a sympathetic smile.

I took it silently, coated my lips, then gave it back to her.

"Everything okay?" she asked.

"Of course," I said, aware that a little frown had crept over my forehead. "I should get back up there. With Jac."

"Sure, sweetie."

Mrs. Gray said nothing. Her forehead was creased and her expression bleak. She walked gingerly, favoring her right foot.

"I think Mrs. Gray might be able to use that Band-Aid, though," I said, and turned and jogged back up toward Jac without saying anything else.

Jac and Ben were walking and talking cheerfully right through the center of Britches. I envied their inability to be distracted by him. And I envied Jac in her ability to casually chat with Ben.

"Look!" Jac pointed, as I reached her right side.

The path ahead opened up onto a broad patio with flagstones, centered around a large stone building with a red roof, flanked by four flags. Opposite the building the flat paved area ended in a guard rail, where the world seemed to drop off. Through the mist, the outlines of the city and glimpses of the river were visible. The three of us, well, the four of us, to be precise, walked across the patio to the railing.

"Imagine what you could see on a clear day," Ben said.

I looked over at him, and he looked back at me. Those sparkling eyes, not so much brown as four different shades of it. When Ben looked at me, I really felt seen. How could I have been this boy's lab partner in bio for an entire three days and failed to notice those amazing eyes?

Britches was peering anxiously over the rail. He turned frantically to Ben.

"Hochelaga est là? Là?"

Ben was standing with his hand on a large stone on which there was a plaque. He suddenly looked half asleep.

"...Sanguenay n'est pas loin. Là-bas, il y a des riches...Il y a beaucoup de riches...."

I looked around wildly. Britches had fallen silent. Jac was snapping pictures, and Ben was still zoned out. There was no one else around.

"...c'est bien pour la roi. Pour la France. Je dois prendre Sanguenay pour la France!"

Oh, boy. I was hearing voices again.

It was like the supernatural world was conspiring to make sure I could not get friendly with Ben. Imagine trying to have a conversation with someone while a morning talk show blared in your ear. Difficult. And whether it was because I could never get a word in edgewise, or he ended up thinking I was a total nut job, it seemed the supernatural was going to win.

"Let me take a picture of you two," Jac

said. "Hey, Ben — snap out of it. Picture! Come on you two, squish together."

Did the girl never let up?

But let's face it. I didn't want her to let up.

I pretended not to want to be photographed, praying Jac would loudly insist.

"Oh, no…," I said. "Not of me. Just take one of —"

"Kat Roberts, stop arguing with me and get in the picture!" Jac commanded.

I immediately and happily complied.

I stood next to Ben, smiling expectantly at Jac's camera. I shifted my weight, and our shoulders brushed. *Please let Jac take forever to take the picture*, I prayed silently.

"Smile! Got it!"

Ah well. The important thing was there was now a picture of me and Ben together. If it turned out my eyes were closed or my smile malformed, I would throttle my friend. Steal her Twixes and Mars Bars and replace them with vegetables.

"Okay, guys," I heard, just as a fat raindrop landed on the ground. "Unfortunately it looks like the chalet is closed for cleaning."

Another drop fell on my head.

"And the weather is kind of turning," Sid continued.

As if Sid's statement had been a command rather than an observation, the sky opened up and it completely and totally began to pour.

"So we should probably head back for the coach," Sid called. According to Sid, like Tim, we were traveling on a motor coach, not a bus. I liked the sound of it.

Brooklyn and Shelby were screaming and covering their heads as if sulfuric acid were falling from the sky. They took off at a run, and the Random Boys followed them, imitating their girly running and hooting at the top of their lungs. Yoshi produced the world's smallest umbrella from his backpack and handed it to his sister. She squeezed under it with Alice and Indira. The rest of us were content to quick-march back down the path. More dignified than running, and besides, it was only water.

We reached the leprechaun-mobile in a quarter of the time it had taken us to walk to the top of Mont-Royal. Sid stationed himself by the door, counting each one of us as we got on the bus. Tim the Motor Coach Operator looked startled and rumpled in his seat up front, as if he'd been in a deep sleep.

Jac and I had gotten separated from Ben on the jog down. I tried not to look for him as I brushed the water out of my hair. What

I did see, after glancing in his general direction, was that Britches had gotten on the bus with us, and was sitting next to Beige Girl.

I could just kill him. Except he was dead already.

Chapter 8

Our next stop was supposed to be the Biodome. It was a short bus ride (or rather, motor coach journey according to Tim and Sid) from Mont Royal, so I did not have to address the problem that two ghosts had now taken up residence in the seats across the aisle from my soul mate, who had safely, if not dryly, made his way to the bus.

"Look," Jac was saying, waving the display screen of her digital camera around in front of me. "Look! Are you looking?"

"I can't look if you keep moving it around,

Jac," I responded, shifting in my seat. Next time Jac really ought to give me the window seat. Ben had a window seat. At least then I would have the same view he had.

"Give it," I commanded, taking the camera from her and examining the image on the screen.

It was actually a really nice picture of both of us. Ben's eyes do this amazing thing when he smiles — it's like some kind of light is projecting out of them. If that wasn't enough, his dark eyebrows angled slightly down on the outside, making him look very compassionate, like he was ready to listen to all your problems.

He wore his black hair in a short brush cut, which had remained unaffected by the stiff breeze up at Chateau Mont-Royal. His olive green windbreaker was zipped up most of the way, giving him a sweetly sporty look and complementing his almond complexion. I could have stared at his picture for a very long time. If the appropriate technology existed, I'd have had the photo tattooed on the inside of both my eyelids.

I have to say I didn't look so bad myself. Jac had snapped the picture just as Ben's shoulder had brushed mine, and there was a happy glow on my face. My smile looked real, probably because it was. Maybe it was just wishful thinking, but I thought we looked really nice together. He wasn't too tall — only about three inches taller than me. Even the deep purple of my thick fleece seemed to go nicely, without being matchy-matchy, with Ben's jacket.

The whole picture was so glorious I could almost, but not quite, ignore the small sphere of light that appeared slightly behind and over our heads. Most people would dismiss it as a smudge of dust on the lens, perhaps lit by a stray ray of sunlight. But I knew better. The round light object was a spirit orb — the manifestation on film of a ghost.

Britches, I presumed.

"So you have to go show it to him!" Jac said, nudging me enthusiastically.

"I so do not!" I replied, in my best I-mean-it voice. "That would be really lame, Jac."

"You're right," she said. "I'll just send it to his phone."

She got up on her knees and leaned over the back of the seat.

"Ben. Hey, Ben!" she called to him where he sat in his usual seat, three rows back, as I repeatedly hissed the word *no*. "What's your cell number? I want to send this picture to your phone."

I heard Ben's voice, and numbers. *Why why why?* I thought. It seemed like Jac could never leave anything that related to Ben Greenblott and me alone.

But giving it a little more thought, it *was* a good picture. Maybe it wasn't the worst thing in the world to let Ben see that we sort of looked cute together. I let the outraged expression stay on my face, but inwardly I was a little happy. Very a little happy.

"Sent it," Jac said, plopping down next to me. "And now we have his number."

"*You* have his number," I said. Jac reached into my fleece pocket and pulled my phone out.

"Stop," I said quietly and unconvincingly. She held her phone next to mine and pushed some buttons.

"Now you have his number, too," she said with satisfaction.

I put my head on her shoulder.

"Oh, Jac," I said. "After all this, if it turns

out he doesn't like me I'm going to lose my mind."

"He likes you," Jac said. "I can feel it. You saw how he was smiling in that picture."

True.

"But if he doesn't," I pressed. "Or worse, if he ends up liking someone else, I'll die."

"Then you can haunt him," she said cheerfully.

"Helpful," I responded.

A commotion, comprised entirely of female voices, erupted in the rear of the bus.

"What's going on?" Jac asked. "Can you see? Is the bathroom overflowing?"

Jac's suspicion of the on-bus facilities was obviously going to be an ongoing theme of our trip.

I stuck my head around my seat and peered down the aisle.

Shoshanna Longbarrow was standing at

the very back of the bus, flanked by Stacy and Shelby, who were trying to stand up in their seats like a couple of royal guards. Phil was snapping photographs of them on his cell phone, while two of the Random Boys tossed an inflatable ball back and forth over his head. Shoshanna had a scowl on her face that said very clearly that some unfortunate soul had displeased her. Intrigued, I leaned farther into the aisle and strained to hear what was going on. Suddenly, a figure leaned out and blocked my view, waving to get my attention. It was Britches.

"Hochelaga?"

I shook my head and gestured at him to go away. After a moment, he withdrew into his seat.

"But I don't see why," I heard a familiar voice whine.

"Because. I. Said. So. Brook, I don't know

what is *up* with you recently, but you are really getting on my nerves," Shoshanna declared.

Now I could see Brooklyn. From the way her enormous purse was partially wedged behind Shelby's purse I guessed there was some sort of seating dispute going on. It might sound silly, but when you're a Satellite Girl, who sits where is of crucial importance. Periodically emotional violence erupted as people angled for a better position in the pecking order. It was like watching a documentary on Animal Planet about the only watering hole in the desert.

"But Shelby was —"

Shoshanna raised one hand, traffic cop–style.

"Just move," she said. Then without another word she sat down in her back-row seat, removed Lacy Fowler's iPod from Lacy's own hand, stuck in the earbuds, and began pumping her foot to a fast beat. Brooklyn hesitated, then grabbed her bag from Shelby's seat and turned around. Our eyes locked.

And I shouldn't have done it; I know I shouldn't have done it.

But I smiled, and not in the kind of way that's meant to be nice.

Chapter 9

The Biodome loomed in front of us like a spaceship. Tim the Motor Coach Operator pulled obligingly close to the front entrance, and we scurried into the building through the driving rain. The structure had been built less than twenty years ago, and the exhibits were all centered around animals. So, there was a very good chance this portion of our trip would be ghost free. Plus, I was a sucker for anything having to do with a rainforest — and in the Biodome they had recreated one and imported the appropriate animals.

Sid had produced his clipboard at the ticket counter, and various forms and bits of paper were being exchanged. Mrs. Redd stood nearby nodding as if her life depended on it. It was then that I noticed we were missing some key people. I pushed my way through the students and tapped Mrs. Redd on the elbow.

"*Oui, Katuh?*" she said, Frenchifying my name by adding a syllable to the end.

"Um, Madame Rouge, my mother…the two parent chaperones, my mom and Mrs. Gray. They're not here."

"*Non,*" she said. "*Elles ne sont pas nécessaires ici parce que—*"

"Could we maybe do this part in English?" I asked, adding a bright smile because grown-ups often like that sort of thing.

"Ah. We are here to speak French, Kat. But in any case, we're giving them a bit of a break while we're at the Biodome. Sid and I will be with you at all times, of course, but this is a completely enclosed facility. None of you can accidentally wander off or get lost, so your *mère* and *la mère de Jac* have gone for a coffee."

"Gone for a coffee?" I asked. "Like, a coffee in the same place? Together?"

"*Oui, ensemble*," she declared. When I stared blankly, she added, "Yes, together."

"I...well. Okay. Thank you."

I walked back to Jac, taking a stealth note of Ben's position as I went. He had obtained a map of the Biodome and was studying it intently.

"Jac, something weird is going on," I said.

"Yeah, why isn't he over here with us?" Jac asked, a little too loudly. She was wearing a strawberry-red fleece that was absolutely

enormous on her and somehow comple-
mented her floppy red hair. I took a moment
to remind myself of her adorableness before
shushing her.

"Not so loud, jeez," I said. "I'm not talking
about Be...about that. It's our moms. Apparently, they went for coffee together."

Jac looked weirded out.

"Together? As in with each other?"

"I know, right? What can they possibly
have to talk about?"

"Nothing," Jac said quickly. "It's stupid.
Forget it."

Forget what? Jac was acting very weird.
Then again, she often acted weird.

I started to ask, but was interrupted
by Sid.

"Okay, guys, so we're gonna go in. I know
you've all done your reading so you know that
there are four complete ecosystems recreated

right here in the Biodome. We're gonna start in the rainforest.

"There's only one way to go, from one exhibit to the next, and once you've left one you can't go back in. So take your time, drink it all in, and we'll meet up at the exit of the last exhibit by the gift shop in two hours. And no flashes on the cameras, please, because they aren't so good for the animals."

Our little herd began moving forward. Mikuru and Indira were chattering excitedly with Yoshi close behind them, scanning the rest of the crowd like a Secret Service agent. The Random Boys were imitating some sort of primate, or maybe they always behaved that way in museums. Who knew? Phil was recording everything on a tiny video recorder. Ben, still holding the map, was waiting to the side for a break in the crowd.

"Kat Roberts, it's time," Jac said.

"Whuh?"

"Are you going to let Ben Greenblott walk all by himself? It's ridiculous. You're dying to hang out with him. So, do something. Go and ask him to walk with us. It's just the Biodome; it isn't … brain surgery."

I took a deep breath and looked Jac in the eye.

"I can't," I told her.

"You can," Jac said. "Look at Brooklyn."

I did. She was applying a heavy coat of lip gloss and casting pointed looks in Ben's direction.

"She looks like she's getting ready to go talk to him," Jac said.

Now, there was no way Jac could know what Brooklyn meant to do. But truth be told, it did seem possible.

"Do you want that to happen?" Jac

pressed. "Ben's so nice, if Brooklyn attaches herself to him he might not be rude enough to tell her to get lost."

A terrifying thought.

"Okay, I'll do it," I said.

"Good," Jac said. "Let's have a code word in case you want me to leave you two alone."

"We don't need a code —"

"Glockenspiel," Jac said. "If you want me to buzz off, say *glockenspiel.*"

We did not need a code word. Of that I was sure. Not today, anyway. But since the chances of my ever figuring out how to use the word *glockenspiel* in a sentence were slim to none, it probably didn't matter.

"Okay," I said. "Do I look —"

Jac reached out and untwisted my earring. She grabbed a section of my hair on one side and put it in front of my shoulder. Then she reached into her bag, produced a tiny bottle, and gave me a squirt of the same perfume she'd spritzed me with at the hotel.

"Now," she said.

It's good to have the kind of friend who can perform this sort of appearance tune-up without hurting your feelings. I gave her a smile, and as the line moved forward I veered off in Ben's direction. He glanced up from the map as I approached, then did a double take when he saw it was me, which was kind of… well. Gratifying.

"Hey, Ben," I said.

I'm sorry. I was very nervous. It was all I could come up with.

"Hey, Kat," he said, and the greeting just sounded so much cooler coming out of his mouth. "Are you psyched? I know it sounds nuts, but I've wanted to visit a rainforest all my life."

I stared at him for a second, truly surprised.

"Me too," I said. "But, actually, seriously me too. I mean … I …"

I was out of words. And in spite of the fact that I had not even approached the word *glockenspiel*, Jac was nowhere to be seen.

"I guess this is as close as we're going to get," he told me.

What?

What?

I must have been staring with my mouth hanging open.

"To a rainforest," Ben said. "For the time being. I guess this is as close as we're going to get to a real rainforest."

I am the stupidest person in the world, sometimes. This was one of those occasions.

"Exactly what I was going to say," I lied.

The line had been moving during my

display of stupidity, and we found ourselves at the threshold of the rainforest. The entrance was a small tunnel hung with long strips of rubber and plastic that you had to brush through. It was like going through a car wash. Without the car.

When we emerged on the other side, I came to a full stop, overwhelmed.

The energy was delicious. The air was thick and warm and moist. It smelled of earth and leaves and water. There were unfamiliar sounds all around — bird calls and hoots and rushing water. It was as if we were on another planet entirely. I felt more than saw Jac at my elbow, which meant that she was either coming to my rescue or bored with leaving me alone with Ben.

"My hair is going to frizz," she said.

"Jac, it's like…it's like paradise!" I exclaimed.

"If you say so, Voodoo Mama," Jac said. "Seems to me there could be all kinds of aggressive rainforest-type insects in here. Based on what I've seen in the movies, they're probably supersized. I need a bug detector. Do you think they sell them in the gift shop?"

"Will you look at that tree?" murmured Ben.

I was already looking at it. It was like the great-grandfather of trees — warm and wide and strong and reaching far up into the air where I could see movement on its branches.

Ben walked over and placed both hands on the trunk, and he leaned in close so his face was almost touching the bark. I was on the verge of asking Jac to secretly snap a picture of him doing this delightful thing when I began to hear voices again.

The voices were male, there were a number of them, and they were speaking or chanting in a guttural language so foreign to me I couldn't even begin to identify it. And unless there was some odd, avant-garde bit of performance art taking place somewhere in the Biodome, the voices were not coming out of my time, or my space.

But they weren't ghosts. Not the way I usually experienced them. My eyes were open. People were moving about, pointing at things and taking pictures and walking and talking, and there were no spirits cavorting amidst them. But I could hear this strange chanting clear as a bell. What was happening to me?

Should I be scared?

I had gotten a half minute or so into serious consideration that I might be experiencing some sort of mental breakdown — because let's face it, hearing voices is never the best sign — when I heard a dainty scream.

Shoshanna was standing a few feet away from me pointing at a spider — a very large, hairy spider that may well have been carrying some sort of weapon. The fact that the spider was displayed under Plexiglas and had all the appearances of being, you know, dead, had not done anything to alleviate Shoshanna's distress at having seen it. The Satellite Girls instantly surrounded her, at least three of them did, making sympathetic sounds of disgust and covering their faces with their hands. Both of the sporty Random Boys joined the group, alternating between mocking the girls' fear and offering anti-spider protection services.

Brooklyn had been left out of this comfort-fest and stood off to one side, unable to squeeze into the crowd and equally unable to tear herself away from it. When it became obvious that the sea of Satellite Girls was not going to part and welcome her in, Brooklyn took a few confused steps in the opposite direction. She caught sight of Ben, his hands still on the tree, and she walked over and stood behind him, clearing her throat. When he didn't move, or acknowledge her in any way, she spoke.

"Ben," she said, more loudly than she needed to. She shot me a look to make sure I was listening.

"Ben," she repeated, "Can you help me with my camera? The thing won't —"

Ben held up one hand in a "wait a minute" gesture. He remained with his back to her, hands on the tree. Brooklyn stood for an uncomfortable minute, then looked in another direction, like someone had called her name. Which no one had.

She took a step back from Ben, weighing her options. Then her eyes met mine. And they narrowed. I wasn't going to pretend I didn't see. Brooklyn was in the middle of one huge incomplete forward pass. Why should I make it less embarrassing than it was? Brooklyn should have picked another boy to bat her eyelashes at, plain and simple.

"Bummer about that camera," I said.

"Be quiet, Spooky," Brooklyn said. She came right over to me and got in my face a little.

"I almost didn't come on this trip because of your gypsy mother," Brooklyn said.

What?

"That's right. My mother was very concerned about your mother being a chaperone. Actually, most of the mothers were concerned about it. It's inappropriate. A fortune-telling crystal ball reader has no business supervising children. And I think it's my duty to make sure Ben has all the facts about your family."

My face flushed furiously with rage. Once, when Brooklyn had said similar things about my mother, I had gotten so angry I recited a fake incantation and made her believe I was conjuring up spirits to haunt her. I knew it was wrong for any medium to deliberately cause fear, and I'd promised both myself and my mother I'd never do it again. But I certainly enjoyed the memory of Brooklyn running away from me in terror.

"How come you're not hanging out with Shoshanna?" I asked innocently, as if the subject of my mother had never come up. "Oh yeah, I forgot. She doesn't like you anymore."

"Of course she likes me," Brooklyn snapped.

"Really? I thought people who liked each other usually hung out together. Even talked to each other. My mistake."

"Shut up," Brooklyn said. "I'm out of here.

I'll catch Ben later, make sure he gets up to speed on our local coven of witches, sorry, I mean your family."

"You do that," I said, scowling. "If you can get him to give you even a minute of his attention."

"Oh, I can do much better than that," Brooklyn declared. She tossed her high-maintenance hair and walked off, navigating around the Satellite Girls like she hadn't noticed them, and making a beeline for the oversized toothy fish display.

I felt uncomfortable. Ben obviously wasn't high on Brooklyn, but I knew when she put her mind to something she could be extremely driven. Particularly when that something would make someone else upset.

I used to think people like Brooklyn Bigelow existed only in books and movies. By which I mean people who took pleasure in deliberately causing difficulties or unhappiness for others, simply because they found it fun. But Brooklyn Bigelow was sadly real. Maybe she had low self esteem. Maybe her parents were mean to her, and she was merely turning her pain outward and dulling it by being cruel to others. Maybe Brooklyn Bigelow was miserable on the inside.

Frankly, I didn't care. I hated her.

Chapter 10

Ben, Jac, and I were way ahead of the group by the time we emerged from the Antarctic ecosystem, where Jac had squealed with delight at the antics of the various penguins waddling with dignity and sliding on their stomachs into pools of water.

"They're just like little people," she exclaimed.

"Like which little people exactly?" I asked her, suppressing a laugh.

"Little…partygoers in formalwear milling about and frolicking," Jac declared.

"Oh right, *those* little people," I said with a grin.

We were waiting for Ben to finish up at the cash register. He had picked out a beautiful book about rainforests, which I would have wanted to borrow from anyone but especially wanted to borrow from him. ("Read it together," Jac had already coaxed.) He had also purchased a small lump of rock thought to be thousands of years old that had actually come from Antarctica, where it was dug up by a geologist.

"I guess we can go back into the lobby," I said. Brooklyn, having nothing better to do, had just wandered into the gift shop and was sullenly examining a display of sterling silver spider monkey earrings. I couldn't relax around Ben when I knew Brooklyn was just waiting for another chance to jump in and berate me. Or worse yet, to breathlessly inform Ben that both my mother and I were mediums.

I didn't need that.

"Let's go grab some seats in the lobby or the café," I said.

"Excellent idea," Jac agreed. Her current plan was to agree with all my suggestions, to encourage what she had now apparently decided was just a long wind-up to Ben's and my marriage ceremony.

"Good thinking," Ben said. "I could use a break. I'm on sensory overload."

We walked out of the gift shop and down the hall leading back toward the café and ticket counter. It was late enough in the afternoon that the lobby had cleared out. Everyone who was visiting the Biodome today was already inside.

As we walked, I got the distinct feeling we were being followed. Stupid, too-much-time-on-her-hands-not-enough-gray-matter-between-the-ears Brooklyn! But when I shot a look back, it was not Brooklyn Bigelow that was following us. In fact, it was not a person at all.

It was a penguin.

Okay. Take a deep breath.

I peeked over at Ben. He was holding the Antarctic rock up to show Jac.

"Gack," said the penguin.

Another deep breath.

Since I felt I could assume that the Biodome was not in the habit of allowing its many penguins to visit the gift shop with guests, or to leave the Antarctic ecosystem at all, there were only two logical possibilities left. First, that through multiple system failures and human error, one of the penguins had managed to escape undetected. The second possibility was that this penguin was in fact a former penguin.

Which meant I was seeing my first real animal ghost.

Okay, yeah, I'd glimpsed a few pioneer-era oxen by the local history museum back when I first started seeing spooks, and there might have been a couple of horses, too. But I'd only seen them fleetingly, from a distance. They weren't interested in me, just in pulling their covered wagon full of pioneers in the direction of the Oregon Trail.

"Gack," the penguin repeated, flapping his little wings in the air for emphasis.

"What are we doing?" Jac asked. "Are we going back to the gift shop?"

"Hang on a second," Ben said. He was still

holding the rock in his right hand, but his gaze had gone distant. "Did anybody hear something funny?"

There was a long silence. My mind raced.

Jac caught my eye and mouthed "what's happening." I shook my head. I didn't know yet.

"Gack gack," the penguin said.

"There it was again," Ben said.

"I didn't hear—"

"Jac, about the gift shop…," I said hurriedly. "I forgot to…I meant to—I was going to see if they had any, um, books."

"They have books," Jac declared.

"Specifically, though, about…glockenspiels."

Jac's eyebrows shot up.

"Oh my gosh, that's wonderful!" she said. "I mean, a wonderful idea! They might have a really good glockenspiel book there. I'm going to go back and check right now."

She dashed down the hall as if she were being chased by wolves.

Ben gave me a curious look.

"Why would the Biodome gift shop carry a book about glockenspiels?" he asked.

Yeah, I definitely should have asked Jac what a glockenspiel was before accepting it as a code word.

"Gack-uh-gack," said the penguin. He looked at me intently, and his little penguin eyes glittered, as if he were enjoying our conversation.

I took a deep breath. I was developing a theory about Ben, and if it were right, it could mean everything. And if it were wrong, he might never talk to me again. But I had to take the plunge.

"I hear it," I said. "The sound. I hear it too."

Ben looked at me closely.

"You do." It was a statement, not a question.

"Yes. It's like...gack."

"Gack," the penguin confirmed, rounding his little white belly proudly and shifting from side to side on his yellow feet.

"Yes, it is," Ben said. He cocked his head to one side, which I normally would have found adorable but right now I was too nervous to fully appreciate. "Jac didn't seem to hear it, though."

"Correct," I said.

"Kat...," Ben began. And I did take a good second or two to appreciate what a glorious thing it was to hear Ben Greenblott say my name with his very own lips.

"I feel like you're trying to tell me something," he said.

I looked at my shoes. I heard Brooklyn Bigelow's voice inside my head, taunting me, threatening to inform Ben about my mother and me being mediums, so sure that when he found out what a freak I was he'd run all the way to the United States border and never look back.

But the fact was, some things were beginning to add up. When I first heard disembodied voices at the Notre Dame Basilica, Ben had been standing nearby with his hands pressed on an old wooden pillar. I was sure of that. It hadn't seemed important at the time, but I distinctly remembered it because I distinctly remembered every single thing Ben Greenblott did or said in my presence.

Then in Mont Royal Park, when I'd heard more voices speaking in French, Ben had been standing with his hands on stone. And in the rainforest ecosystem, he had been pressing his palms against the big tree when I heard chanting. Now he was holding an Antarctic rock, and not only could I hear a penguin, I could see one.

My mother says there are no coincidences — only red flags that the Universe throws our way to alert us to something significant that is happening. Without knowing anything more, I could only make my best guess. And my best guess was that Ben Greenblott was clairaudient.

He could hear supernatural sounds and voices that others could not. And somehow when he was channeling something, I picked up the sounds, and sometimes apparently the images, as well.

The question was, did he know it?

"Gack."

Ben looked at me, and I nodded.

You have to tell him, I commanded myself.

You have to tell him you see spirits. You have to tell him he's gifted, too. You have to do it right now.

I looked full into his face. His lovely dark brows had pushed together in concern and confusion, and his eyes looked worried. He ran a hand over his hair, never once taking his eyes off mine. I had to tell him. I owed it to him.

If he didn't already know about his gift, he might think he was nuts hearing those voices. What would I have given to meet another thirteen-year-old who saw ghosts when it started happening to me last year? If I cared about Ben Greenblott, and I think you've picked up on the fact that I did, I needed to be honest about who I was, and what I could do.

"Kat, do you know what a clairaudient is?" Ben asked suddenly.

My mouth dropped open. It's a bad

habit of mine when I'm speechless. I'm sure I looked hideous, but I just let it hang there for a second. Wide open. Total gaping maw. Attractive.

"Have you heard of clairaudients? I can't even get into what you believe, not yet. Just if you know what I'm talking about. They're, um…people who can…"

"I know what a clairaudient is," I said, quietly. "A clairaudient hears spirit voices. *You* are clairaudient."

Now Ben's mouth dropped open, but he closed it right away.

"That's right," he said.

"You tune into the energy of a physical object, and when you touch it, you get sensations or sounds or even voices associated with the history of that object."

He was leaning toward me, listening very intently. It was kind of distracting.

"That's exactly right," he said. "How can you know that?"

And he waited, expectantly. And I knew now that it was okay.

"I'm clairvoyant, Ben," I told him. The sentence sounded so weird coming out of my mouth, like I was quoting some cheesy science fiction space opera. "I see spirits, and I can communicate with them."

Ben whistled under his breath. He did not make a move to bolt for the U.S. border.

"I knew there was something," he said. "I could tell that when I was picking up on something from an object that you somehow heard something too. I just didn't know how, or if you were consciously aware of it. Or how it could be happening."

"I was surprised, too," I said. "I've never heard just voices before. When it happened in the cathedral, I couldn't figure out what was going on. Between you and me, I was starting to wonder if I was losing it."

Ben laughed.

"I can imagine," he said. "So if I'm picking up something and you're standing nearby, you can actually hear the same thing?"

I nodded.

"And in this case not just hear it," I said, pointing at the penguin, which gave me an inquisitive look and opened its beak slightly.

"What? Do you see something there?" he asked, looking back and forth from the place the ghost penguin was standing to me.

I laughed.

"Yep. It's a penguin. A really cute one, too. You don't see it?"

Ben shook his head, looking sorely disappointed.

"Let's try something. Put the Antarctica

rock in your backpack or your pocket — somewhere you won't actually be touching it."

Ben took his navy blue backpack off, unzipped it, and tossed the rock inside.

The penguin blinked, gave me a quizzical look, then disappeared.

"It's gone," I said.

Too bad, too. It was a really cute penguin.

"Wow," Ben said. "It disappeared from your sight as soon as I broke contact with the rock?"

I nodded.

"And so you're clairvoyant? Kat, that's amazing. I've never met an actual clairvoyant before. When did you — how did you... I'm sorry. I've just never..."

His voice trailed off, but I knew exactly what he meant. He'd never met anyone that was different in the way he was different before. Until now.

Until me.

"But if you can hear what I hear, why can't I see what you see?"

"I don't know," I said. "Maybe you can, and we just don't know how to make it happen yet."

Ben looked at me expectantly, like he was waiting for a suggestion. And actually, I had one.

I looked at my watch.

"We have fifteen minutes before we're supposed to meet up with the group," I said. "I have an idea. Can you come out to the bus with me?"

I know. It sounded crazy—me asking a boy to sneak out to an empty bus with me. It was totally and completely against field trip rules; Sid had made it very clear we weren't supposed to leave the Biodome without the group for any reason. But this was no ordinary situation, no ordinary boy. Not even the bus, at this point, was ordinary.

"Sure," Ben said.

My heart jumped a little.

"Hi!" came Jac's voice.

"Hey," I said.

"I couldn't find the, uh, book I was looking for, but look what I got!"

Jac held out a small stuffed penguin with a sweet face and a stylish tuft of hair on the top of his head.

"I couldn't resist buying him. Isn't he adorable? His name is Osbert; it says so right here on his name tag."

"He is adorable, Jac," I said. "Listen, Ben and I need to run outside for a second. Alone."

Jac's eyebrows practically shot clear off her forehead like little rockets.

"It's not…we just need to…it isn't," I stammered.

Jac pulled me to one side. "Does this involve ghosts?" she whispered.

Oh.

See, if I said yes, Jac would want to come. If I let her think perhaps this was more of a glockenspiel moment, she would send me off alone with Ben with her handprints firmly on my back.

"No," I said. Could she hear the guilt in my voice? I was lying to my friend.

Jac raised one hand in the international "stop" position.

"I don't require any explanation," she said primly.

I took a breath. I'd explain later, but right now there was no time.

"If Sid does a head count and we're not back, tell him we…"

"One of us dropped a cell phone and we went back in to look for it," Ben suggested.

"Got it. Cell phone." Jac said. Then she winked at me.

The girl was relentless.

"We better hurry," Ben said.

We darted out the front door together, me and Ben Greenblott.

Voices, spectral penguins, and pouring rain notwithstanding, it was turning out to be an outstanding afternoon.

Chapter 11

Tim the Motor Coach Operator was fast asleep in the front seat with a huge cup of coffee balanced between his knees. We had to stand in the rain banging on the door for about a minute before we could wake him, by which time we were soaking wet. Tim opened the door and closed it after us, took a slurpy sip of his coffee, and immediately went back to sleep. He seemed completely unconcerned with what we were doing there, and that was fine with me.

"Come back here," I told Ben, leading the way down the aisle. "To where your seat is."

When I got to Ben's row, Britches stared up at me expectantly.

"*Hochelaga?*" he asked.

Beige Girl gave me a brief glance, then resumed staring out the window.

"Okay," I said, stepping to the side to make room for Ben and gesturing toward the spirit seats. "Do you see anything there?"

Ben looked carefully.

"No," he said. "Is there something there?"

"Two people," I said. "Spirits. The first one, I call her Beige Girl because, well, her skin and her sweater and her hair are all kind of that color. She got on the bus at Notre-Dame. Hasn't said a word. There's a big guy sitting next to her, who looks about eighteen or nineteen and is wearing sort of old-fashioned beat-up clothes. He started tagging along at Mont-Royal and then followed us down to the bus from there. I call him Britches."

Britches looked up when I said that.

"*Hochelaga?*" he asked. Britches looked like even he was getting tired of hearing that word come out of his mouth.

"He keeps saying the same word, and I don't know what the word means," I said. "Sometimes he says other stuff, but it's in French, I think. I can't really make it out."

"I didn't hear it," Ben said. He looked genuinely disappointed.

"I guess it's because these two are purely spectral," I said. "There's nothing physical from that time period that you could touch now to connect with them."

"So you can see them, and they can see you. Can they see each other?" Ben asked.

"From what I can tell, no," I said. "Either

they don't see each other at all, or they register each other sort of lumped in with the rest of the people on this bus, the ones who can't see them. They seem to divide the world into two types: regular people, and mediums. Well, not just mediums. People with abilities. Like you. They're aware of you too — they seem to know you are picking them up somehow.

"Britches showed up at Mont Royal when you were touching a rock up on the overlook. I heard other voices there too, also speaking in French. But these two are apparitions — they don't have anything physical with them. But they seem drawn to you, Ben. I mean both of them have come and sat near you. How long have you known you were clairaudient?"

"All my life," Ben told me. "My mother called the voices my 'imaginary friends' when I was little. I thought all kids heard the same voices. Then my mother went from being amused by my imaginary friends to scared. When I got older I learned to keep what I heard to myself. I didn't learn there was a name for what I was, or that there were other people like me, until I was twelve."

We stood together, dripping in the aisle.

"There must be some way…," Ben began.

I heard voices outside the bus, saw Tim sit up and lean forward, and heard the hiss of the bus door opening. I made a guilty jump away from Ben, but my wet sneakers connecting with the slick aisle while I was off balance caused me to lose my footing and slip forward, toward Ben. He reached out and grabbed my hands with his, stopping me mid-fall. I yelped with surprise.

Britches drew back from the commotion.

"*Hochelaga*," Britches muttered, sounding irritated.

Ben did not let go of my hands right away.

The sensation of his palms on mine was electric. For a moment I forgot that the bus door had opened. I wanted to tell Ben I was okay, that he could let go now.

But I didn't want him to let go.

"*Hochelaga*," Ben whispered.

"What? You heard it?"

"Is that what Britches has been saying?"

I nodded. My face was hot, and I didn't need a mirror to know it was bright red.

"I heard it!" Ben exclaimed. "Just now —"

"What in the world is going on?"

Ben and I let go of each other's hands and spun to face the front of the bus.

Mrs. Gray was standing there with her hands on her hips, and she looked, in a word, scandalized.

"What are the two of you doing here? You're breaking the rules! Is Jacqueline with you?"

I shook my head miserably.

"No, it's just the two of us," I said.

Plus these two dead people.

"We weren't doing anything. I mean, we weren't doing anything wrong. Bad. We were just…"

"Just what?" Mrs. Gray gestured with her head as she asked the question, sending her velvet headband slightly askew.

"There was something on this bus I really needed Ben to see," I said.

"And that was what?"

Ben and I exchanged a quick look.

"I can't tell you," I said.

"And you expect me to —"

"Mrs. Gray, please," I said quickly. "You and I spent a whole week together at the Mountain House. Which I really, really appreciated. You said I was a good friend for Jac. I think you even started to like me. I'm not a troublemaker, or a liar, and neither is Ben. I just can't be more specific about what we were looking for on the bus. There's sort of, other people involved. Who can't speak for themselves."

Someone else had gotten onto the bus behind Mrs. Gray. It was my mother. I wasn't sure whether to feel elated or mortified.

She looked back and forth between Ben and me and Mrs. Gray. Tim the Motor Coach Operator was sitting in the front row unabashedly watching what unfolded, his gaze bouncing back and forth between us and the chaperones like he was at a tennis match.

"What's going on?" my mother asked.

"This boy was in the back of the bus with your daughter," Mrs. Gray said. "Kat says she is unable to give an explanation for what they were doing here. This violates school policy."

She turned back to Ben and me. "You could both be suspended if your teacher finds out about this."

What? First of all we weren't in the back of the bus, we were just beyond the middle of the bus. And Mrs. Gray was going to snitch on us? It was pretty clear we weren't doing anything. The Motor Coach Operator was right there the whole time.

"Let me find out exactly what's going on first," my mother said. "Give me a moment."

She walked toward me, clearly confused. When she got to the place where I was standing, she glanced over to the seat where Britches and Beige Girl were sitting. Her eyes widened just a tiny bit, then she took my elbow.

"Come sit in the back with me for a sec. Will you excuse us?" she asked Ben. He nodded, his face flushed scarlet. We moved past him to the very last row — the heart of

Shoshanna-land. She made a gesture, and I sat down next to her.

"Kit Kat. I think I understand, sweetie. I think I know exactly what's happening."

I felt an odd surge of relief. My mother knew me better than any person in the world other than Jac, and Jac had known from the outset that I really liked Ben. Why wouldn't my mother have noticed, too? We could have normal mother-daughter stuff after all, about boys for once instead of ghosts.

She would understand. I liked a boy and I had gone somewhere with him I technically wasn't supposed to go for totally innocent reasons. We'd talk it out. Just like a normal mother and daughter. Normal.

"You've attracted several apparitions that seem to be drawn to you and are currently haunting this bus," she said very quietly.

Welp. Forget normal.

"True," I said, looking at my shoes. *Please don't let Ben be able to overhear this conversation*, I thought. *I'd like to be the only clairvoyant he knows, even if it's just for the day.*

"And Ben, he's picking up something, too, isn't he? They both seem to gravitate to him," she said, running a hand through her damp hair. Her hands were thin, I noticed. All of her was very thin. Another way in which we were not alike.

Fine. The conversation would be about the supernatural side of the situation, not the way I felt about Ben. Phantoms before feelings and all that.

"Yes," I replied. "We were trying to figure out if there were any conditions under which he could see them, too. We had just walked out here. Then Mrs. Gray showed up."

Like the Secret Police, I added as a silent afterthought.

My mother nodded thoughtfully.

"I think I can smooth this out," she said. "Let me talk to Jac's mom."

"What were you guys doing, anyway?" I asked.

"Getting coffee."

"You. And Jac's mom. Just shooting the breeze?" I asked. It came out more sarcastic than I meant it to. My mom was wearing faded jeans and an ancient oversized cashmere sweater with a hole in the elbow that I think once belonged to my grandfather. Jac's mom was wearing pleated khaki pants, a white and pink pinstriped oxford shirt, and a belt with a gold shell as a buckle.

"She just needed somebody to talk to," my mother said.

I gave her a curious look. If the subject had been medium-related my mother would not have mentioned it at all. I actually suspected that Shoshanna Longbarrow herself had contacted my mother last year when her grandmother died. But Mom refused to talk about it, even to simply confirm that some kind of communication with the grandmother had taken place.

That was the main reason I thought it had. Well, that plus the fact that Shoshanna had been much...well, I'm not sure I'd use the word *nicer*. But she'd sort of seen to it ever since that the Satellite Girls not torment me.

"Let me have a word with Jac's mom, okay? Why don't you and Ben go back to the lobby? It's just about time for the *rendez-vous* now."

"Okay," I mumbled. I felt embarrassed and uncomfortable and couldn't get off the bus fast enough.

My mother walked up the aisle to where Mrs. Gray was standing.

"I think I understand what they were looking for," my mother said quietly. "And I also understand why Kat feels uncomfortable about sharing the details. I can only say they weren't breaking any school rules — other than simply being on the bus in the first place."

Mrs. Gray glanced in my direction.

"I appreciate what you...our talk. I do. And I don't want to make a mountain out of a molehill. I just don't want to give anyone special treatment," Mrs. Gray said. She sounded hesitant — I think she was already off the warpath.

"You're quite right," my mother told her warmly. "But in this instance, it's more that you know the student in question. I think Kat's earned your trust. And I'm sure both these kids can honestly promise you this won't happen again."

"We promise," I said quickly.

"We promise," Ben added, staring at his sneakers.

Mrs. Gray still looked uncertain.

"Thank you so much," I said. Because sometimes it helps to thank somebody for something they haven't done yet. It worked like a charm here.

"Well…you're welcome," she said. "But please let us not find ourselves in this situation again."

"We won't," I assured her. "We'll get back to the group now."

"Come on," I said to Ben, ignoring Beige Girl and Britches.

I glanced at my mother, who gave me a smile and a nod. What was going on between her and Jac's mom?

We brushed past my mom, past Mrs. Gray, and then past Tim, who was watching all of us like we were an episode of his favorite television show, and got off the bus. Mrs. Gray followed us off the bus and stood with her hands on her hips, all Captain Authority. I realized she intended to stand there and personally watch Ben and me walk back to the Biodome, so we couldn't make a mad dash for, oh, I don't know, Quebec City maybe.

"Are they friends — your mom and Jac's mom?" Ben asked.

"I wouldn't say that," I said. "Jac and I are best friends, which sort of makes them friends-in-law whether they like it or not. And I don't think they like it." Or hadn't until today, when they suddenly became coffee chums. What was up with that?

But there was no time to think about that now. As we approached the front entrance to the Biodome, I realized we had an audience of one. Brooklyn was standing under the awning, her cell phone flipped open, staring at us.

Great. She had obviously seen everything that went down — the parent chaperones getting on the bus, me and Ben being frog-marched off the bus, and Mrs. Gray standing there like the Enforcer, making sure we committed no additional crimes on her watch.

Brooklyn looked utterly enraged.

I kept my mouth shut as the two of us walked past her to the door. There is an old saying about the fury of a woman scorned, and Brooklyn Bigelow was definitely feeling scorned by Ben Greenblott. There was nothing that needed to be said — the girl looked like she was already going nuclear.

Jac was standing right inside the door and practically pounced on me.

"Perfect timing!" she whispered. "Sid just

called out his first 'Okay, guys,' and he hasn't even done a head count yet!"

"Not so perfect," I whispered back. I drew her to one side and Ben wandered over to the water fountain to give us some space. "Our mothers happened to get onto the bus while we were there."

Jac's mouth dropped open.

"Did my mother go postal?" she whispered.

"She started to," I said. "My mom talked to her — kind of explained without explaining that we weren't breaking any of the rules she thought we might be breaking. Mom could see it was a ghost stuff we were dealing with, not boy-girl stuff."

Jac's face fell.

"You told me it wasn't ghost stuff."

"I didn't exactly say —"

"I asked you if it involved ghosts, and you said no. You lied to me, Kat!"

Had I?

"I didn't...I didn't mean...There was no time to argue, Jac, and I know how excited you get about ghosts and I didn't want you to...I mean, Ben and I needed to...I needed to see if he—"

"No, forget it," Jac said, glowering. She leaned close to me and whispered. "I'm the one who's been trying to get the two of you together. I'm the one who made you talk to him in the first place. And now you're just trying to get rid of me so the two of you can go ghost hunting alone."

"That's not true at all, Jac," I said. Where was this coming from?

"It is true," Jac said. "You'd rather hang out with him than me now. I should have known this would happen. Things never stay where you want them to. People never stay where you want them to."

"What are you talking about?" I asked.

Jac said nothing.

"Jac, what —"

Brooklyn swept through the lobby door and shot me a triumphant smile. I knew exactly what was going inside her lima bean of a brain. She had the one thing that might both get back at me and win her readmittance to the inner sanctum of Satellite Girls — a bit of juicy gossip.

I turned back to where Jac had been standing, only to find her gone. She had taken herself over near where Sid was standing, and was rooting around in her bag. She pulled out a pack of gum, glanced up and saw me watching her, and turned in the other direction. I didn't know what to think. Was all this just because Ben and I had gone to the bus without her?

The lobby door opened again, and my mother and Mrs. Gray walked in. My mother caught my eye and gave me a little nod. I couldn't get used to the sight of them together, like they were ... friends or something.

And I was starting to feel self-conscious standing all by myself. Ben was still over by the water fountain, fiddling with his phone. Jac was reading the back of her pack of gum, apparently enthralled with the information. How long was she going to stay mad at me? And why didn't Ben come over? Maybe he had never liked me in the first place, not *like*-liked. Or if he had, our brush with amateur law enforcement had scared him off.

My phone beeped, and I pulled it out. The screen informed me that I had a text message.

The sun exploded back into my world. Jac must have given Ben my number! I'd have to thank her — when she was speaking to me again.

Avoiding J's mom. See u back at hotel? By soda machines?

OK, c u then, I texted back, trying not to grin at Ben like SpongeBob.

Ben snapped his phone shut and smiled at me for a moment, before walking over to the Story of Biodome display.

It is difficult to momentarily find yourself the happiest person on the planet at the same time that your best friend is mad at you. I couldn't stand it. I made a beeline for Jac.

"Please don't still be mad at me," I said to her.

She looked like she was trying to ignore me, but she gave up quickly.

"Give me one good reason," she said, pressing her lips together.

I gave it some thought. I could go for serious or glib. I decided on glib.

"Your feet are cuter than mine," I said.

Jac was very vain about her feet. They *were* cuter than mine, and she liked to be reminded of it.

"True," she said, "though I'm not sure it's a good reason not to be mad at you."

"You won't take pity on a poor girl with ugly feet?" I asked.

"They're not ugly," Jac said. "Just a little bony."

"My pinky toes are crooked."

Jac gave me a sympathetic look.

"Only a little," she said. "Not so much that anyone else would notice."

"Thank you," I said.

"Anytime. What's new?"

"Brooklyn saw me with Ben and gave me the Super Death Ray look. And Ben texted me to meet him by the soda machines when we get back."

Maybe I shouldn't have added the part about Ben. But Jac looked pleased. Whatever had caused her mood swing, she was over it.

"Serves Brooklyn right," she said. "Bad karma. What are you going to wear to the soda machines?"

"I don't know. What do people normally wear to the soda machines?"

"Let me think about it," Jac said. Then she looked off into the distance, and I could tell she really was mulling over what clothing we had back in our room.

She was the most outstanding friend in the universe. Even if her mother had briefly considered having me suspended.

Chapter 12

"I bet you anything she's back there talking about me," I whispered to Jac, who was bouncing Osbert the penguin toy on her lap like he was a baby.

"Brooklyn?" Jac asked.

I nodded.

"She was practically drooling to get the story of me and Ben on the bus out to the world."

"Let her tell it," Jac said. She poked me in the arm and I looked at her. Her small, delicate features were arranged in a serious expression. "Do you care?"

"I don't know. Nobody likes to be talked about. She's probably spinning the bus thing into some ridiculous drama."

"So let her," Jac declared.

"I just wish I could see what was going on."

Jac fumbled around in her purse, pulled out a Mars Bar, a tube of something called Smarties, and a white and blue rectangle that said CADBURY on the side, then found what she was looking for.

"Here. Open this, angle it back, and spy away."

I took the little mirror and held it slightly over the aisle. With a few adjustments, I could see the back row perfectly. Brooklyn was indeed standing over Shoshanna talking rapidly and waving her hands around in the air. Once or twice she pointed toward where I was sitting. Then she laughed so hard I thought she might rupture something and capped off the performance by putting her hands on her hips and shaking her head.

Then my view was suddenly blocked completely. It was as if a person had materialized right behind me out of thin air.

Which they had.

"I do hope you are not applying cosmetics."

I turned gingerly toward the voice.

Standing at my elbow was a tiny, bird-thin woman with white hair pulled back neatly but far too tightly into a bun. She wore a navy blue suit and sensible shoes. On her right lapel was a pin that said TOUR GUIDE, and below that a name: VELMA.

"Cosmetics violate the rules, and are

inappropriate for someone of your youth. When you become a lady and the time arrives when it is acceptable to wear a touch of rouge and a little lipstick, you will do well to remember that less is more."

I was pretty much speechless. Though it occurred to me that if she were going to make personal statements about others, Velma might do well to consult with a hair care professional.

"Very well then. I will resume the tour. Do you have any questions about the site of the future Biodome?"

She waited with her lips pursed. Looking at her bun made my head hurt. Something told me I'd better produce a response.

"The future Bio..." My voice trailed off into a mumble. "What?"

Velma sighed.

"The site of the future Biodome, my dear,

which we have just visited. I do wish young people were better listeners. Do you have any questions about it?"

I shook my head.

"It is impolite to shake your head. Yes, ma'am or no, ma'am is the proper response."

"No, ma'am. Actually, yes, ma'am," I whispered.

Velma looked a little pleased.

"What is your question?"

"How long until the Biodome is finished?" I whispered.

"That will not be determined until after our Olympic Games are over, dear," Velma said.

"Thank you," I whispered back.

"Now put your compact away. It is not ladylike to check your reflection in public."

I snapped the mirror shut and handed it to Jac.

"Done already?"

I held a finger up in the just-a-second symbol. I counted to three, then took a quick peek behind me.

Lady Velma was taking a seat.

Next to Ben Greenblott.

"I can't believe this," I said.

"What did she do?"

"There's *another* one."

Jac waited, leaning slightly toward me. When I didn't continue right away she made a "get on with it" circular motion with her hand.

"There are now three ghosts on this bus," I whispered.

Jac's eyes shone.

"Who? Where?" she whispered. She was clutching the tube of Smarties in one hand. As she waited for me to answer, she removed the top of the tube, and shook a few of the M&M-like candies into her mouth.

"She's a tour guide. She's obsessed with manners. Jac, when were the Olympic Games in Montreal?"

"That's easy — 1976," Jac said.

So Lady Velma was from the seventies. My mother called it the Misunderstood Decade. Lady Velma was quite possibly the Miss Understood in question.

"She kept telling me I had to be more ladylike."

"Well, it wouldn't kill you," Jac said.

I gasped and she bent over double laughing.

"Joke. Joking!" she wheezed. She had really cracked herself up. She only reined it in when a few of her Smarties tumbled out of the tube and onto the ground.

"Rats," she said. "I knew I should have bought more of these when I had the chance."

"She sat down next to Ben."

Jac's little red eyebrows shot up.

"Are you kidding?"

"I'm serious," I said. "I feel like half the ghosts in Montreal are trying to come between us."

"That actually sounds romantic," Jac said.

"Not to me."

"Okay, guys," I heard. I straightened up and gave Sid my attention. He was standing at the front of the bus. Before he could continue, Lady Velma came up the aisle and stood in front of him.

"All right, young ladies and young gentlemen," she said.

It was the weirdest thing. Sid was a good head taller then Velma, and I could see the rest of him — his leather jacket, his black and white fringed scarf — right through her navy blue suit.

"We're about to get back to the hotel," he said.

"In approximately two minutes we will be arriving at our lodgings," said Lady Velma.

"You guys have some time to hang out in the hall or in your rooms and chill out, or whatever."

"Please use this time to freshen up. A clean tourist is a happy tourist," Velma said.

"You know the rules. Stay where you're supposed to be, and keep it under control. Do your school proud," Sid finished. He plopped back down into his seat.

"Comport yourselves like proper young ladies and gentleman at all times. You are little ambassadors of your nation."

Lady Velma surveyed the seats solemnly. Her gaze rested on me for a moment. Then she walked regally toward the back of the bus and sat down next to Ben again. I had been watching her go, and when she sat down, Ben caught my eye. He waved. I waved back, and Lady Velma instantly stood up, like a gopher popping suddenly out of its hole.

"Young lady, please refrain from waving," she called to me. She gave Ben a disapproving look. "Particularly to a young gentleman. It does not behoove you."

Behoove me?

Ben looked perplexed and completely unaware that a spirit from the Disco Decade was sharing his seat.

"I'll explain later," I mouthed.

I saw Lady Velma's head snap toward Ben, and I dived down in my seat.

"Man, she is one uptight old broad," I whispered.

Jac was too busy pouring Smarties into

her mouth to ask what I meant, and anyway, we were pulling up to the front entrance of our hotel.

The hotel containing the hall containing the vending machines contained in the alcove where I had agreed to meet Ben Greenblott in mere minutes.

Chapter 13

"How do we make them go away?"

We. He said we. As in the two of us. I'm part of a "we."

I stared intently at a can of Diet Pepsi in the vending machine to help keep my expression neutral.

"It's different with every spirit," I said. "Plus they have to want to move on. Well, first, they have to realize that they're dead. Actually, before that they have to realize you can see them. Oh, it's complicated."

We had taken cushions from the couch,

which tended to consume people and make it impossible for them to stand back up when they wanted to, and were sitting on them on the floor below the window.

"No, I think I understand," Ben said. "So we're going to have to come up with a completely different plan for each of these ghosts."

Oh. There was that "we" again.

"Yeah," I said.

"How do you start?"

"You figure out everything you know about them in life. Lady Velma, for example. We know she's a tour guide, obviously, and we know she's stuck in the seventies."

"Drag," said Ben.

"Yeah. And Britches. I have a theory that he's from Jacques Cartier's time. I'm not sure what time period —"

"Sixteenth century," said Ben.

"Okay then," I replied.

I had forgotten Ben was a brain, due to my focus on the rest of him.

"And he's looking for someone named Hochelaga. So that's a place to start with him," I said. "Beige Girl I have no idea. She could be from the sixties or from last year. She doesn't speak, though I'm sure she knows I can see her. It's hard to know what she wants."

"Maybe if we can help Britches and Lady Velma move on, she'll get the idea and offer us a clue," Ben said.

"Exactly," I said.

We. We. Wheee.

Sorry.

"And once we've figured out how to help them, we'll have to find a way to get back on the bus when no one else is there without getting ourselves expelled."

"Yeah, Jac's mom doesn't exactly belong

to the 'bake fudge and hug it out' school of parenting. Or chaperoning," I added.

"I hear Jac is like a prodigy level cellist," Ben said.

I nodded, filled with pride.

"She is," I said.

"I heard her last year, that one time that she played — remember? At that pre-dance talent show thing Shoshanna Longbarrow threw together."

Oh, I remembered it okay. I lured Jac there under false pretenses knowing she hadn't played her cello in a year, and tricked her into performing a duet with the ghost of a student who needed her old teacher to hear her in order to be set free. It occurred to me that I could tell Ben about it — tell him about all the things that had happened — the dark entity that had stalked Jac's mom at the Mountain

House, the lost boy in the abandoned house next door to mine.

But I was here with Ben now, with a bus downstairs rapidly filling with ghosts. Maybe the other stories were best left for another time.

"Wait, I think I have an idea, actually," Ben said. "This person Britches is looking for. Hochelaga, right?"

I nodded.

"That might be a good place to start. Do you have wireless Internet?"

I shook my head. I didn't have a laptop either, but it seemed pointless to get into that much detail.

"Okay, well, I do. I'm going to get online and do a little research about that time period. Google that name. Maybe I can come up with something."

"That's a great idea," I said. And it was, except for the fact that it would involve Ben going back to his room, where I was not allowed to follow. I needed a task, too, so Ben could see that I was a busy medium, not merely a lovesick eighth grader.

"I'm going to read through some of the handouts about the Biodome and the Olympic Complex," I said. "Maybe I'll get some insight into Lady Velma that way."

"Great," Ben said, flashing a grin that should definitely be qualified as a lethal weapon. "Let's see if either of us can come up with something before final check-in."

He was already standing. Raring to go.

Or raring to get away from me?

Stop it, I told myself. *It was his idea to meet you here in the first place. Don't be ridiculous.*

"I won't," I said.

"Won't what?"

Oh, great. Had I said that out loud? There *was* something worse than hearing voices. It was hearing your own voice, saying something you didn't mean to say.

"Won't give up till I've figured it out," I said.

"That's my girl," Ben said. Then he turned on his heel and walked quickly toward his room.

My? Girl?

My head was swimming.

It's only an expression. Stop planning your wedding, my inner voice commanded.

Then another inner voice immediately began singing "My Girl."

Sometimes the inside of my brain is a really terrible place to be trapped.

I stood up slowly, still nursing a bit of a Ben-induced head rush. Then something truly hideous, something spine-tingling and

100 percent evil, loomed into view in front of me.

Brooklyn Bigelow.

"Talking to yourself?" she asked. "You and Cello Girl are a couple of freaks. Do you know what you get when you put two freaks together?"

"I don't want to tax your math skills, Brooklyn," I said. I held out my purse. "Here. I think there's a calculator in here somewhere."

She made an ugly face, on top of the ugly face she usually had.

"Rumor has it you got busted for going through people's backpacks on the bus," she said. "I guess when you can't afford stuff of your own you're tempted to steal from people who can."

I knew she'd make it something bad.

"Actually, Ben and I didn't see any backpacks on the bus," I said, emphasizing Ben's name.

"Everybody knows the truth about you, Kat. Everybody. Knows."

"Enjoying the food in Montreal, are you?" I shot back. "Looks that way. Hey, listen, I could probably conjure up the spirit of a personal trainer for you, no problem. Get you some help with your muscle tone issues. Should I go ahead and do that for you? It's no problem, really. I could have someone following you around 24/7."

I wasn't supposed to make threats like that, I know. It sort of violates the medium's code of conduct. But the step back that Brooklyn took was so gratifying.

"Shut up," she said. "You're a sick person, you know that? Just like your mother."

I pressed my lips together tightly as the blood rushed to my face. I had no snappy comeback for that. When Brooklyn brought my mother into things, I just saw red.

"I've been thinking about your mother, actually," Brooklyn said. "Since I've been seeing her every day and stuff. I mean, I keep as far away from her as I can. Everybody does. But people can't help noticing those disgusting old thrift store clothes she wears, and stuff. Not much money in the spook business, huh?"

I glared at her.

"That is my grandfather's sweater."

"What? Oh gosh, is your grandfather a medium, too? That is so, so sad. I actually feel really sorry for you, Kat. I mean, you can't help being what you are, can you?"

"I guess that makes two of us, Brooklyn. What are you doing out here anyway? Oh, right, I remember now. You're not welcome in Shoshanna's circle right now. You know, once you're out it can be very hard to get back in. Remember Lanie Bingham? Shoshanna kicked her out, and that was the end for her. She ended up in the math club," I added meanly. "Before she transferred to another school, that is."

"What makes you think I'm out?" Brooklyn said. Her eyes had gotten huge and dark, like a lemur I'd recently seen in *Extreme Bush Babies* on Animal Planet.

I hadn't really thought that, actually. Only wondered about it after Brooklyn ended up sitting by herself on the bus after spilling the Kat and Ben story to Shoshanna. But judging by Brooklyn's expression, I'd hit kind of close to home.

"Oh, everybody is saying that," I lied. It was so easy to lie to Brooklyn. Something else I had to be careful about.

"Everybody as in who?" she asked. She

looked more scared by this than she had by the prospect of a dead personal trainer being assigned to her.

"You know. Everybody," I said. "Actually, I think they just feel really sorry for you," I added, borrowing another one of Brooklyn's lines.

"Yeah? Well, that's ridiculous. Anyway, if there's anyone people feel sorry for, it's Shoshanna Longbarrow."

"Is that a fact?"

I turned around. Shoshanna was standing behind me, in the doorway of the alcove. She was barefoot, wearing tiny low-riding jeans and a little Aeropostale T-shirt with a monkey on it. Her glossy dark hair hung perfectly straight around her face. Her pink lipstick was impeccably applied. Her expression was unreadable.

"I asked you a question, Brook. Why is

everybody feeling really, really sorry for me?"

I looked over at Brooklyn, half amused and half embarrassed for her.

Well, maybe not half. She had brought it on herself, after all.

"No, Kat said that," Brooklyn said suddenly. "I was just repeating it back to her."

"That's lame," Shoshanna said. "You're usually better a much better liar."

"I'm not a … She's the one who …"

"No, I'm done," Shoshanna declared. "I am so done with you, Brooklyn."

"Sho, let's just go and —"

"Which word didn't you understand? I'm done. That's your cue to go away."

Dang. I wasn't even close to being a Satellite Girl, but I could feel the authority in Shoshanna's voice. This girl was a born leader. At least, in a country of eighth graders.

Brooklyn made a sort of half-whine, half-protest. After a moment's hesitation, she ducked her head and stormed past both of us. Shoshanna watched her go, shaking her perfect head.

"Whatever," Shoshanna said. The word didn't seem to be directed at me, or at anyone in particular. But the cans of Diet Pepsi in the vending machine looked like little silver soldiers standing at full attention.

"So," she said, looking at me.

"So," I repeated.

Shoshanna nodded, like I'd said something very deep and unusual. She rummaged around in her pocket, pulled out a Canadian dollar bill and some change, and inserted it in the soda machine. The machine accepted Shoshanna's dollar on the very first try. Even the vending machines did her bidding.

Diet Pepsi in hand, Shoshanna turned

toward me. I assumed she'd simply walk back to her room, but she stood where she was.

"So you and Ben," she said after a moment.

I didn't know where this was leading, so I just looked at her. I tried to keep my expression totally blank.

"Did they really bust you two on the bus?" Shoshanna asked.

She looked curious and almost sympathetic. So I nodded.

"That bites," Shoshanna said. "Did you get detention or something?"

"No. We weren't really doing anything. Just talking. It was no big deal. They basically let us off with a warning."

"Cool," Shoshanna said. "He's nice, that guy Ben."

"Yeah, he is," I said.

"Cool," Shoshanna repeated. "Anywayz. Catch you later, Kat."

And she walked out of the room, clutching her Diet Pepsi while all the other unchosen cans watched jealously from the vending machine.

I really had no idea what had just gone on between me and Shoshanna Longbarrow.

But whatever it was, I couldn't wait to tell Jac.

ॐ

When I got back to the room, Jac was lying on her stomach, watching television from the bed. The floor was littered with blue and silver wrappers.

Before I could even open my mouth, Jac turned to me with a rapt expression on her face.

"They have the. Most. Amazing. Shows. In Canada."

"Aren't they the same as —"

Jac pointed at the television as if it were a case of Godiva chocolate.

"They have this program called *Stargate*," she declared breathlessly. "It is the most outstanding thing I have ever seen. I am totally going to marry Colonel Jack O'Neill," she added.

"Jac, they —"

"See, they're in this secret Air Force base underground and there's this Stargate you can dial like a phone and it makes a wormhole and it can send you anywhere in the universe to another planet with a Stargate!"

"But Jac —"

"Shhh! I can't miss any of this. There's a *Stargate* marathon on this channel all night, and I'm going to watch as much of it as I can stay awake for. We only have one more day in Canada, Kat."

She looked suddenly glum. "I really don't want to go home," she added.

The boys of *Stargate* disappeared and were replaced with a box of laundry detergent. Jac's face went blank. She looked odd — not like her usual self.

"Is something bugging you?" I asked. "Are you still mad at me?"

Jac sat up and fussed with the pillows, then lay back down again.

"I was never mad at you," she said. "I'm just...ugh. Something happened I didn't tell you about."

My heart started beating faster.

"What?" Jac looked the same way she did when our mothers went out for coffee.

She sat up again, and put one of the pillows in her lap.

"My father kind of lost his job."

"What? When?"

I had only met Jac's father a few times, because he traveled a lot for his computer work, and when he was home he was usually napping or holed up in his study.

"He told my mother the night before we left for Montreal. I almost didn't get to come, Kat. She wanted both of us to stay home. I think if the trip fee wasn't nonrefundable, I wouldn't be here."

"Jac, I'm so sorry. What…what's going to happen? What will this mean for you?"

"I have no idea," Jac replied. "Nothing good, that's all I know."

"I'm really sorry," I repeated, because I didn't know what else to say. "I'm sure he'll find another job soon, right?"

"I guess," Jac said.

"He will," I said.

"Anyway, that's the mystery of our mothers having coffee solved. Knowing my mother, she probably won't tell any of her friends what happened. But…"

"My mom is a sympathetic ear on this trip, but she's not in her…in her circle back home." I said.

Jac nodded.

"When we get back I guarantee you my mother will act like they never talked at all. That's actually bugging me almost as much as the deal with my father."

"Jac, you know my mom. She doesn't get her feelings hurt over stuff like that — she's used to it. People come to her hoping she can contact some departed relative, but then they pretend like they don't know her in the supermarket because they're embarrassed. She's got a pretty thick skin."

Jac looked like she wanted to say something, but didn't.

The boys of *Stargate* reappeared on the television.

"They're back!" she said, flopping down on her stomach again.

And because she was my best friend and I understood her so well, I knew Jac was done with the subject of her father and his job. That's just the way Jac was—she liked to shut unpleasant things out, and act like they weren't happening. My mother called it compartmentalizing. I resolved to keep a closer eye on my friend. But I'd also play it her way—the subject of her father was completely closed.

"I have to read about the Olympics," I said. "Where are those booklets and handouts we got?"

Jac pointed toward a bag with her foot, then shushed me.

"Quiet," she commanded. "Colonel O'Neill is talking."

I got the bag, pulled out the contents, and settled on the other bed. Before I started reading, I glanced over at my friend.

"Hey, Jac? You know, they do show *Stargate* in the U.S., too."

Jac let out a scream so loudly euphoric I doubt anyone needed a wormhole to hear it clear across the galaxy.

Chapter 14

It was our last day in Montreal, and the schedule was packed. Mrs. Redd was making sure we got every penny's worth before starting on the four-hour trip back home late that afternoon.

Jac and I got off to a late start, mostly because she had turned the television back on in the morning and discovered the *Stargate* marathon still going strong. I had waited with her for an episode to end, then we rushed downstairs, dragging our suitcases, just as

Sid was starting to head through the lobby to look for us.

"Okay, guys, I thought we were gonna have to leave without you," Sid admonished. "Leave your bags there, and go ahead and get on the bus. Everybody else is already on."

"No breakfast?" muttered Jac darkly.

I was about to remind her that it was her fault we had missed breakfast, when she produced a bar-shaped item from her bag.

"You're having a candy bar for breakfast?" I asked her.

Jac looked aghast.

"Please! No. It's a protein bar, Kat."

I took a closer took at it.

"It says Chocolate Caramel Chaos on the wrapper."

Jac pointed at the back.

"Protein. Bar. This is health food. Want one?"

I held out my hand and Jac slapped the bar into it, fishing a second one out of her bag. If our bus slid into a ditch and we were trapped there for several days before being discovered, I had no doubt we could all live very well off the snack collection Jac carried around with her.

I glanced over at Mrs. Gray as I climbed onto the bus. Given what I now knew, it seemed that what I'd taken to be uptightness in her expression was perhaps more worry than anything else.

"Good morning, Mrs. Gray," I said brightly.

She looked up at me, seeming surprised that anyone was speaking to her.

"Oh — hello, Kat."

"Last day," I said. Then I smiled at her, but I cut it short. If I started getting too talky and friendly with Mrs. Gray, she might figure out what Jac had told me.

I waved at my mother and took my regular seat. Jac got on the bus last, barreling down the aisle without a word or look at either of our mothers. This wasn't the first time I thought Jac went a bit hard on her mom. It wouldn't kill her to be polite — and unlike the cello drama of last year, this situation certainly couldn't be blamed on Mrs. Gray. But Jac ignored her and plopped down next to me.

The bus ride was short and miserable. Short because we were going to a part of Montreal that was just ten minutes away. And miserable because when Jac and I got on the bus, I saw that Brooklyn Bigelow was giving it another shot and had sat with Ben Greenblott. With my Ben Greenblott. The other half of my We.

It was a crime and an outrage, and Ben didn't look too thrilled about it, nor did Lady

Velma, who was wedged in between the two of them, partially transparent and providing a glimpse of Brooklyn's hipper-than-thou fitted leather jacket. Brooklyn was violating just about every makeup and conduct code Lady Velma had, and she sat blissfully unaware of the lecture she was receiving in one ear, as she blathered on to Ben, flipping her hair and blinking her eyes like a confused monkey.

I couldn't look, and I told Jac I didn't want to talk about it. I wasn't stupid — it was pretty obvious Ben wasn't into Brooklyn. But that didn't make the fact that she was sitting there batting her eyelashes at him any easier. I slumped glumly in my seat until we reached our destination. I was the first one off the bus. I shot down the aisle so fast my mom was still in her seat zipping her coat up. She raised a questioning eyebrow at me, but I just shook my head a little and brushed past.

It was just starting to rain as I stepped onto the pavement. According to our schedule, our first stop was the City Hall, and an ancient remnant of the wall from the original fortified city. Unwilling to be standing around when Brooklyn descended with her stupid triumphant stares, I headed toward the public square next to the old building. I was wearing a bright green slicker over my fleece and the City Hall was close. Sid would be able to see me, and if there was any doubt, my mother could pick me out from a mile away, if necessary.

I kept my head down as I walked. The square was mostly deserted. I passed a young couple laughing, completely oblivious to the bad weather. As I approached the square, I saw a man with dark, wild hair and a beaky nose who gave me a bad vibe. I looked away, and put some distance between us as I tried to walk past him. His gaze on me was so intense as I neared him that I couldn't help glancing over. He looked astounded, and enraged. He quickly stepped into my path. As a reflex, though I immediately knew he was a ghost, I stopped.

"Qui êtes-vous? Qu'est-ce que vous regardez?"

The energy coming off him was dark and angry. I did not have the time, energy, or experience to tangle with him. I turned and began walking in a different direction.

But he was in front of me again, and I could not bring myself to walk straight through him.

"Qu'est-ce que vous regardez?"

I spun around 180 degrees and back-tracked. I didn't get more than three or four steps away when he blocked me again.

"Arrêtez et répondez-moi."

That one I understood. Stop and answer

me. And something else he'd said—I knew more or less what it meant. What did you see? He was asking me what I had seen.

"Back off," I said loudly, because this was no time to worry what I looked like to anyone watching. "Get. Away."

He only glared at me, and stepped closer. A force seemed to roll off him—something cold and sharp like the blade of a new knife.

I was afraid of him.

Someone grabbed my arm and I screamed.

"Kat, Kat, it's me."

Ben was standing behind me, his hand still on my arm. He was staring at the man like he couldn't believe his eyes. I wanted to say something, to explain, but I couldn't, and Ben seemed to have figured out the crucial parts, anyway.

Dead guy. Bad.

The guy lunged forward suddenly, and

Ben pulled me back and away. There was a set of steps leading down toward the old wall, and we ran down them. We stopped at the bottom, both of us out of breath, and Ben let go of my arm.

"Are you all right?"

I nodded, and Ben looked back up the staircase.

"I couldn't see him until I grabbed your arm. But I could tell something was wrong."

"He's...different. Really bad energy. I was scared."

"So was I."

For the first time it hit me that I was standing there with Ben, who'd just pulled me out of the way of a raging ghost, and we were standing around discussing it. When just two days ago the idea of even talking to him seemed hopeless. Life could be strange. And wonderful.

"Can they...can they hurt people?"

"I didn't used to think so," I told Ben. "Unless they scare you into hurting yourself, like falling down a flight of stairs. But this guy...it really felt like he could —"

I felt a blast of cold behind me before I saw him. I whirled around, not wanting to have my back to this ghost for a second.

"*Vous ne pouvez pas échapper*," he hissed.

I racked my brain for anything that my mother or Orin had told me about dealing with angry or menacing ghosts. There had been a spirit of an old man in an abandoned house next to mine who had a similar raging energy. But I hadn't dealt with him at all — I was unable to get over my fear. I had run away, or tried to, and Orin had saved me.

"He's back, isn't he?" Ben whispered.

I felt his hand slip into mine. I couldn't process any of the normal boy-girl hysteria this should have brought. I only felt relieved that I wasn't alone in facing this now. Ben could see him too.

"*Va-t'en,*" I said loudly, using the French familiar form that you'd use with a child, or someone you knew very well. Go away.

Several things happened at once, then. The ghost literally reached for my throat. As he did, Ben stepped forward and threw a punch that would have coldcocked any living person. But the blow passed right through the ghost. The man's hand, however, stayed in place with his fingers at my neck. And suddenly I felt as if he had taken an icicle and plunged it into my throat. I felt a shudder go through my body.

"*Vous allez mourir. Vous allez mourir,*" he hissed.

You will die.

My legs were getting weak. The pain in

my throat felt very real, and was excruciating. I could almost see, from a distance, my frozen body with the ghost's hand at my throat, and I knew that in a moment my knees would buckle.

"*Laissez les vivants touts seules!*"

It was my mother's voice. I had never been happier to hear it.

The grip on my throat relaxed, and I took several wild, off-balance steps back and sat down hard on the pavement. Ben was still hanging on to my hand, and he came down next to me.

My mother and the dead man were face to face. She looked so unthreatening to me — tall but thin as a reed, in jeans and an oversized windbreaker, her blond hair pulled back in a ponytail. He eyed her like a wild animal might size up something it was about to eat.

When he lunged at her the way he had at me, I shrieked.

But my mother did not budge. She stood like a statue, her eyes fixed on his, her lips moving though I couldn't hear what she was saying.

He went at her again, but she was rooted to the spot, and her expression determined but unafraid. It was as if a force field had sprung up around her. This time he began to falter. Now he was the one stepping back.

My mother said one final thing to him, and he turned abruptly and took several steps away. Then he simply blinked out, like a television signal that had suddenly been switched off.

"Whoa," said Ben very quietly.

We were both still sitting on the pavement.

My mother came over cautiously, giving me the chance to speak first.

But I was speechless. I'd never seen her do anything like that. I'd never seen a ghost do anything like that. I had so, so much to learn.

"Are you okay?" she asked quietly.

I nodded. Ben did too. She knelt down next to us.

"I'm sorry I busted in like that, but I saw him following you, and I could tell right away he had the potential to be a nasty problem."

"Do *not* apologize." I said firmly. "That man...that ghost wanted to kill me. And I felt like maybe he could. Could he?"

"He could have hurt you. Maybe worse. He had elements of having been human once, but there was something more, too..."

She glanced over at Ben, and looked

pained. The look she gave me was downright empathetic.

She did know. Not just about the spirit stuff, but how I felt about Ben. She'd probably known from the very beginning, maybe even before Jac had. She'd just chosen to leave the topic alone. And now she looked like she was about to say she was sorry for embarrassing me in front of him. I didn't want my mother to feel like she embarrassed me. Not ever. She was my mother and I loved her, supernatural baggage and all.

"Ben's clairaudient," I said. "If he's nearby, I can hear what he's hearing. And if he… touches my arm or something, he can see what I see."

It only occurred to me after I said it that maybe Ben would have preferred to keep this information private.

"I have a lot of questions," Ben said. "Maybe at some point, like after we get back home…"

My mother smiled.

"Anytime, Ben. Come for a dinner if you want. I don't have all the answers, but I probably have a few. You're not allergic to dogs, are you? Max doesn't shed much, but he's a big boy."

"I love dogs. Dinner would be really great," Ben said. He shot me a sideways glance, and I turned beet red. How long was it going to take to get used to this? It was tiring changing colors all the time.

I heard voices chattering and laughing on the square.

Shoshanna was pointing up at the old City Hall, surrounded by her girls. The Random Boys were attempting to scale a statue like they were in a climbing gym. Mikuru and Phil were comparing iPods, while Yoshi hovered nearby looking uncertain. Indira and Alice were bent double laughing about something while Mrs. Redd waved her little hands at the Random Boys in an attempt to get them down.

"Okay, guys, get off of there now," Sid called, and two seconds later, his word had been obeyed.

Brooklyn stood off to one side, watching Ben, my mother, and me through narrowed eyes. I pretended not to see her. Let her wonder what was going on — there was nowhere for her to spread her gossip at the moment. When we got back I'd worry about what that would mean for me later.

Mrs. Gray was walking with Jac. I raised my eyebrows in surprise. They were talking about something. Jac seemed unaware of anything else going on around her. She kept looking away, and she was scowling. But they were talking. At least they were talking. It was a start.

"Well, we have an opportunity here," my mother said. "Should we take advantage of it?"

"An opportunity?" I asked.

"The bus is empty. Tim went off to get a sandwich. Maybe we should go do a little spirit housecleaning?" she asked with a smile.

"Oh, definitely," I said. "Are you in, Ben? If you want to learn, this is the best way to do it."

I got to my feet. Ben was still sitting on the pavement looking a little stunned.

"I think I already have," Ben said. "Learned a thing or two, that is."

He was even more of a newbie at all this

than me. He had just looked to me for answers that I didn't have. My mother had to rescue us, for pity's sake.

But there was something about Ben that made me feel safe, and comfortable. Like being home.

"And yes," Ben added. "I'm in."

Chapter 15

I tackled Lady Velma first.

"I'd like to help you," I told her.

Ben was standing right behind me—he had to in order to keep his hand on my shoulder so he could see what was going on. But still, it made me nervous having him there. My mother was sitting a few aisles up, silently observing.

"I require no assistance, though if I may be so bold, young lady, I do believe you would benefit from a little attention to your comportment."

Oh. Thanks so much for calling my outfit schlubby with the boy of my dreams standing two feet away.

"You need to move on," I said.

Lady Velma pinched her lips together and narrowed her eyes.

"The next stop on our tour is the site of the future Biodome. We will move on at the time the printed schedule indicates."

"We've already been to the — Lady Vel — I mean, uh...ma'am, your work here has been enormously important."

At least I had her attention now. I tried to pretend Ben was somewhere else. Italy, maybe.

"And that work has made a difference, and you've educated many young people about Montreal, and been a wonderful tour representative for the city. But you're needed somewhere else now. You need to cross over."

"I will do no such thing," Lady Velma declared. "I am a tour guide. That is my service."

She sat down and crossed her legs primly, reaching up to pat her tortuous bun.

"She won't go?" Ben whispered.

Ben's first direct experience with me working as a medium was turning into a train wreck. I was filled with new resolve. I was not going to let a dead tour guide embarrass me in front of my soul mate. I thought furiously, then something came to me in a flash.

"Yes, that is exactly the point — you are a tour guide. You were needed in Montreal, but when you cross over, you'll find they need you much, much more over there."

"How do you mean?" Lady Velma asked.

"This place where you're supposed to be — a lot of people go there every day. But the thing is, some of them get lost. I try to help them from my end, to get them heading in the right direction. But when they get to the other side, sometimes they're really confused. They don't know what to do, they don't understand. If only there were someone like you on the other side—someone who takes charge, who knows how to guide people and explain to them where they are and where they need to go next. It is a very big job, I know, and probably more difficult than what you've been doing here. Maybe it's a bit more than you're willing to take on."

Lady Velma stood up.

"Nonsense," she said. "I never shrink from a challenge. You say people need guiding?"

"They do," I said.

"Where are they?" she asked.

I looked around. This was the trickiest part. It was different for every spirit, and I'd only guided a few over so far.

"There is a light," I said. "When you have the intention of crossing over, you'll see it. Like the sun, but it will speak to you. Not with words—but directly into your heart. You'll feel love coming from it, and intelligence."

The sky was as bottle gray as it had been for the entire trip, but Lady Velma's gaze fixed on a place in the front of the bus, next to Tim's special motor coach operator's seat.

"Yes," Lady Velma said. "I see it. You are quite right, young lady...it is a wise and gentle thing that..."

Her voice trailed off and she stood staring, mesmerized.

"Go toward it," I said. "Let it flow all around you. There will be people there waiting for you."

She took a step toward the light, then paused, and looked around the bus.

"It's okay," Ben said.

Lady Velma stood still, and I was afraid she was going to change her mind and we were going to have to start all over again. But she reached up, unpinned her VELMA tour guide badge, and placed it on a seat. Then she turned and walked up the aisle.

When she reached Tim's bus driver seat, the air around her seemed to shimmer and go out of focus.

"Oh my," Lady Velma said.

Then she took a step forward, and she was gone. There was nothing where she had been standing except the windshield.

"You did it!" Ben exclaimed.

I blushed.

"She wanted to go," I said. "On some level she knew — and she wanted to go."

Ben squeezed my shoulder, and all the breath went out of my lungs.

"Well done, sweetie," my mom chimed in.

Oh yeah. My, um, mom was on the bus too. *Pull yourself together*, I told myself.

"Now Britches," I said, turning around and looking at him where he sat huddled in his seat. He was actually kind of hunky, for a dead guy.

Britches stared at me gloomily. Unlike Lady Velma, I knew he wanted off the bus. But how could I make him understand about crossing over? Especially when he seemed obsessed with this Hochelaga person?

My mother had stood up, and was staring at Britches with her arms folded across her chest. Britches looked from my mother to Ben to me. Frustration was written all over his spectral face.

"He's not looking to cross," my mother said. "He seems very attached to this plane of existence. He wants to go somewhere in our physical reality — he must have left others like himself there. He's attached to it and wants to return. I think he wandered off with you two by mistake, like a moth following a flame."

"But we don't even know who he's looking for," I said.

"I might," said Ben.

"Really?"

"I checked online, remember? And I found something. Hochelaga isn't a person, it's a place. It's the Indian village where Jacques Cartier and his men camped. It was located somewhere on Mont Royal."

Britches stood up. You'll never, ever guess what he said.

"*Hochelaga?*"

Maybe you did guess.

"*Oui, Hochelaga*," Ben told him. "*Vous pouvez rentrer.* You can go back there."

Wow, Ben's French accent was great.

Really great. How terrifically disturbing was that?

"*Le mont*," Ben said. "*Le mont. Hochelaga et sur le mont.*"

Ben was pointing at Mont Royal, visible in the distance. He was showing Britches how to get back.

"*La-bas?*" Britches asked.

"Yes, *oui*," Ben said, nodding in an exaggerated way. He pointed again. "*Le mont.* The mountain or hill. *Hochelaga.*"

"*Ah, oui!*" Britches exclaimed.

"You can go right now," my mother said to Britches. "Look — *regardez.* Close your eyes and see it here," she tapped her head. "See Hochelaga. *Voyez.*"

Britches seemed to understand the half French, half pantomime. I really wanted Britches to get home. In fact, I was incredibly eager to see the last of him. But I was supposed to be the medium here, and yet it was my mother and Ben who had gotten through to the ghost.

Or had they? Britches was still standing there, plain as day, with his eyes closed. I racked my brain for a word in French, but I couldn't come up with it. So I said it in English instead, but I didn't just say it. I felt it. I conjured up the energy, the feel of the word, and I broadcast it in Britches's direction.

"Home," I said.

He opened his eyes for a moment and gave me a quizzical look. Then an expression of understanding crossed his face. He closed his eyes again. And just like that, he was gone.

"That's it!" Ben exclaimed.

"Nice," my mom said.

"What did he do?" Ben asked.

"In his dimension, given that he's basically in an out-of-body state, he can more or less focus on a place and be there. He just has to be able to know that's where he wants to go."

Sounded like *Stargate*.

"So why didn't he just wish himself back to start with?" Ben asked, and I was glad he did, because it sounded better coming from a newbie.

My mother looked thoughtful.

"Maybe he'd never left Hochelaga before. He attached himself to you two because you could sense him, and he followed you. Before he knew it he was somewhere unfamiliar. He probably had no idea what was happening to him. He was probably quite confused and disoriented and decided his safest bet was to stick with a couple of familiar faces."

"Sounds like every day in the cafeteria," I said, and Ben laughed.

The only thing better than making a cute

boy laugh is making a cute boy you are totally into laugh.

Even if your mother is right there.

"So that just leaves Beige Girl," I said.

"Do you know her story at all?" my mother asked.

I shook my head. "I've never gotten so much as a peep out of her. She'll look at me, so I know she can see me. But nothing else."

My mother scooted into the seat in front of Beige Girl, and leaned over the back.

"Hi," she said.

Beige Girl looked at her with mild interest, but said nothing.

"Maybe in French?" Ben asked.

My mother shook her head.

"She's holding a book. Did you see it?"

"No," I said.

"A Montreal tour guide of some kind.

Title is in English. I don't think language is the problem here."

We stood around, trying not to stare at her. I don't think Beige Girl cared. All she wanted to do was look out the window.

Through the same window, I could see our group was beginning to meander back toward the bus.

"I think we're running out of time," I said nervously.

"We may not be able to do anything," Mom said.

"We can't help her?" Ben asked.

"Not everybody wants to be helped. Sometimes, it's better to just wait it out and see if an opportunity presents itself. Maybe something will happen on the way back that triggers something in her. That would be the time to act."

"But we're heading home right after we

eat," I said. "What if nothing gets triggered by then? What are going to do, just leave her on the leprechaun bus for all of eternity?"

My mother smiled at me.

"Things have a way of working themselves out, Kat," she said. "If there's a way home for her and that's what she wants, we'll help her find it. If not now, then someone else will help her, at some other time. In some other place."

I was afraid she was going to start singing. Which, granted, would have been very unlike her.

"Okay, okay," I said quickly. "They're back."

Yoshi was the first one on the bus. He looked at the three of us suspiciously, like he was backstage security for U2 checking for hysterical groupies.

"I'm gonna sit," Ben said. "Hey, thanks, Mrs. Roberts."

"Jane, and you're welcome," she said. "Don't forget about dinner."

Ben went back to his now Velma-free seat.

Me — changing colors again — this time more of a strawberry pink.

"Are you okay?" my mother asked me.

I wasn't expecting the question, and I looked carefully at her face. She looked peaceful, with a tinge of fatigue, and a smidgen of amusement. I felt tears spring to my eyes for reasons I couldn't really pinpoint.

"I'm fine," I said.

She nodded, pulling her old cardigan sweater closed over her neck like she was cold. She leaned toward me and kissed me on the cheek.

"I like him," she murmured.

Then, before the aisles were clogged with Satellite Girls and Random Boys, she went back to her seat.

Jac was right behind Yoshi, craning her neck and leaning around him trying to get a glimpse of me, and to catch my attention. I waved.

"What happened?" she mouthed.

I smiled. It's not like I was going to shout the story across the bus.

When Jac reached me, I would tell her everything.

Chapter 16

Sid had bought pencils that said I LOVE CAN-
ADA on them for every one of us.

"You guys have been really great," he
told us.

"Come to America with us, Sid," called
Phil.

A chorus of "Yeah, come to America with
us!" erupted.

Sid smiled.

"Maybe sometime for a visit, guys. But
my home is here. What can I tell you? I love
Canada."

"And we love you!" Indira yelled. Then she smacked her hand over mouth.

"Okay, guys, be cool for Tim and Mrs. Redd on the way home. E-mail me if you're coming back to Montreal."

Our goodbyes went back and forth another few rounds, then Tim opened the door and Sid got off the bus. He stood waving on the sidewalk as we pulled onto the street to begin the drive back home.

It wasn't until we were approaching the border that the chaos began. That's also around the time that I remembered the squirrelly border guard who had warned me that I would be in major trouble if I tried to bring any thing or *person* back into the United States.

I'm guessing that to him, Beige Girl qualified as a person.

"Brooklyn, I can't believe you're that dumb!" Phil was yelling.

"What's going on?" Jac asked.

"I didn't do anything—it isn't my fault!" Brooklyn was yelling back. "It was like that when I went in—someone else did it!"

A chorus of voices rose together, calling Brooklyn a variety of names. She just stood there yelling back at everyone. It was so weird, seeing Shoshanna and the Satellite Girls *not* coming to her aid. I had called it—Brooklyn had been kicked way out of orbit.

"What is going on, please?" Mrs. Redd asked, plodding down the aisle. The yelling continued. I missed Sid. He would have won instant silence, and a concise explanation.

After a while, the explanation filtered through. Brooklyn had gone into the little bathroom, and when she came out, she had somehow caused the door to lock from the inside. Now nobody could get the door open.

"What if somebody has to go?" demanded Shoshanna.

I was sure Shoshanna wouldn't have to go. She was the kind of person who seemed to never, ever have to go.

"I think I have to go," called Alice.

"I have to go, too," yelled Phil. "Like, really bad."

"I might need to go later," contributed Indira.

"This is terrible," Shelby wailed. "Someone tell Tim."

Mrs. Redd, probably relieved to get clear of the battle zone, immediately did an about-face and marched up the aisle to report the bathroom malfunction to Tim the Motor Coach Operator.

Moments later we were in the parking lot of a fast food restaurant.

The bus exploded into an excited symphony as Tim came down the aisle with a scowl on his face and a large ring of keys in his hand. As he stood trying various keys in the bathroom door, Mrs. Redd stood behind him looking stricken and trying to hush the sea of comments, with no success.

"I don't have a key for this," Tim proclaimed after a number of attempts.

"Well," Mrs. Redd declared. "There are… facilities here. Students, if you need to go to the bathroom, please go inside the restaurant and do so now."

No one stood up.

"I want french fries," yelled one of the Random Boys.

Almost everyone stood up on hearing that, including Jac.

"I'm going to go get an O'Frothy," Jac told me. "Want anything?"

I shook my head. I really didn't. To be honest, I had lost most of my appetite ever since Ben and I had held hands. But, like, in a good way.

"Don't let anything exciting happen while I'm gone," Jac commanded, climbing over me to get into the aisle and beat the rush. She was so small, it was like having a chipmunk clamber over my lap.

"Well, the students can go now, and I suppose we can just pull over again later if someone has to go again," Mrs. Redd told Tim. "I have a cell phone calling chain system in place. I can let the parents know we're going to be late getting back."

"That," Tim declared, "is the least of our worries."

"It is?" Mrs. Redd asked. "What is the most of our worries?"

Tim gave her a frustrated look.

"In about ten minutes after we get back on the road, we're going to reach the U.S. border. We're going to be checked by a border guard. Do you think he's going to have a problem with the fact that we have a locked room on this bus that we can't open to be searched?"

Mrs. Redd thought about this for a good long moment.

"Yes?" she asked.

"Yes," Tim confirmed.

There was really nothing else to say.

We waited in the parking lot for what seemed like an eternity. After the first wave of people got back onto the bus, the smell of French fries inspired a second wave to get off and troop into the restaurant. We were there a good twenty-five minutes before finally getting under way again. Word had spread about our impending difficulties at the border. Tim had taken over, giving a concise lecture on the situation.

"This is serious," he said, in his official Motor Coach Operator voice. "I don't want to hear a peep out of you guys at the checkpoint. No laughing, no smart mouths, no helpful suggestions. We get a guy who's had a bad day, we could be stuck at the border all night, or until somebody kicks that door in, which I'm not paying for."

Jac was sucking her O'Frothy through a straw with such force I was afraid her eyes might pop out of her head. She finally gave it a rest, and nudged me.

"This trip is the best thing ever!" she said.

"Jac, we're about to come under suspicion of smuggling," I said. "We could all be tossed in the slammer."

"Exactly!" she said. "My mother must be having a fit."

I was tempted to go up and see what my own mother thought of all this, but I didn't want to risk unleashing the wrath of Tim. The whole bus had fallen quiet as we pulled into the bus area of the U.S.-Canada border.

Tim got off the bus and went inside a building. Five minutes later he returned with three unsmiling border guards in tow.

Make that two living and one dead border guard in tow.

Mrs. Redd silently handed the package of passports to one of the guards, while a second followed Tim to the bathroom and tried the door.

The squirrelly guard came and stood by me, hands on hips. A set of spectral handcuffs hung from his belt, and I wondered if he was going to try to use them on me.

"All right," announced the guard in the back of the bus. "Here's the deal. Nobody is going anywhere until this door is opened and I see the inside of that bathroom. I don't care how you do it, but I want this door open now."

The bus was as silent as a tomb. Everyone stared at the bathroom. Then everyone stared at Brooklyn.

"It wasn't my fault," she stated.

"Did I ask whose fault it was?" asked the guard. "I don't care whose fault it was. But if you don't get the door open, you can sit here for the rest of your lives as far as I'm concerned."

Bummer. My future with Ben suddenly looked bleak. And very crowded.

Out of the corner of my eye, I saw someone get up. I waited for the border guard to order the student back to her seat, but heard nothing.

It was Beige Girl. She had gotten out of her seat and was standing in the aisle. Looking right at me.

"We can't cross the border until the bathroom door is open," I said to her.

"Yeah, thanks for listening," said the border guard. "I don't think we need a recap."

There were some quickly hushed giggles. I felt like an idiot.

But Beige Girl was looking at me very intently. Then she turned and looked toward the bathroom door. And began to walk toward it.

She walked right through Tim and the border guard. She put her hand on the bathroom door handle, turned it, and pushed.

It swung a few inches open.

"What the—" the guard began. He gave the door a cautious push, and it opened all the way.

"What happened?"

"Did he kick it in?"

"It looked like it just swung open!"

Tim's warning that none of us utter a peep had been forgotten, as everyone offered their own theory for how the locked door had spontaneously become unlocked and opened itself.

There was an outburst of clapping that quickly stopped as the guard stepped into the bathroom and began to examine it.

Beige Girl did not stick around to watch. She began to walk toward the front of the bus.

"Thanks," I said to her when she came even with my seat.

She paused and looked at me.

She was actually quite pretty. She almost looked familiar, in a generic way, just like any old girl you might see in any old place.

"You're welcome," she said.

"I can help you get home," I told her quietly. The back of the bus was still abuzz with the mystery of the bathroom door, so hopefully no one noticed I was talking to air again.

"I can't go home yet," Beige Girl said. "I've lost someone."

"Lost someone?"

She nodded. Her pale eyes looked large and serious. A little sad, maybe.

"We were separated. She doesn't understand. And I won't cross over without her."

"Where were you separated?"

"In Montreal."

Shame she couldn't be a little more specific.

"But how are you going to find one person in all of Montreal?"

"I just need to keep looking," Beige Girl said. "I have time."

I suppose, technically speaking, Beige Girl had all of eternity.

"Good luck," I told her.

She smiled, and when she did a little life bloomed into her face. Who had she lost? Maybe she'd been on a trip, too. Maybe she'd been traveling with her best friend. I would never leave Jac behind, no matter what. I sort of understood Beige Girl now. And I'd be secretly rooting for her.

Beige Girl turned to the squirrely guard.

"Where are the Montreal-bound buses?"

He narrowed his eyes at her for a moment, then pointed.

Beige Girl walked up the aisle, down the steps, and out the bus door. I scootched over to the other side of the bus and watched her walk through twelve lanes of traffic to the northern-bound lanes. There was a big blue bus there, with a huge bowl of oranges painted on the side, and large letters proclaiming VITAMIN C-ANADA. The bulk of the bus blocked my view, but I knew without a doubt that Beige Girl got on it.

It was as my mom said. Some spirits don't want to leave. Some spirits can't. Some spirits choose not to. They're here because they want to keep on doing something that made them happy while they were alive, or because there's something they need to do before they can cross over. Beige Girl had to find her friend.

"Okay, I don't know what the deal was with that door, but the bathroom checks out, and you're good to go," the guard in the back of the bus announced. He and his partner disembarked quickly, walking back into the building shaking their heads. The squirrelly guard scrutinized me, then gave a nod, apparently satisfied that he had completed his duties to the fine countries of Canada and the United States of America.

When the door had hissed shut, and the bus began to rumble forward, everyone began shouting and laughing at once.

"Can you believe that?" Jac was asking. "Everybody back at school is going to flip. That was hi-larious."

It was hi-larious, now that it was over and we were on our way home again.

"Except I think I might have to go to the bathroom," Jac said. "Do you think Tim will stop if I ask?"

"Use the bathroom on the bus," I commanded. "It's not going to kill you."

"It could," Jac said. She looked like she believed it, too.

I took her O'Frothy from her, ignoring her outraged protests.

"Hey," I said. "Do you mind if I go sit... back there for a while?"

Jac stared at me.

"By the bathroom?" she asked.

"No."

"By Shoshanna?"

"No."

I handed her the O'Frothy back. I knew she was playing dumb. She just wanted me to say it.

"Glockenspiel."

"Ahhhhhhhh," Jac said. "Copy that, Commander. Dial the Stargate for Planet Glockenspiel."

She gave me a friendly punch in the arm, which kind of hurt, then she fussed with my hair a little and straightened my fleece.

"Thanks," I told her.

Then I took a deep breath, stood up, and made my way toward Ben Greenblott's seat. Three days ago, on the trip up to Canada, it had been absolutely unthinkable that I would have gone anywhere near him. Now, I couldn't walk to his seat fast enough.

Brooklyn was standing in the aisle, pretending not to notice Ben but at the same time conveniently blocking access to the seat next to him.

I cleared my throat.

"Excuse me," I said.

Brooklyn looked at me blankly. She wasn't going to make this easy. Did she think she could thwart my chances with Ben by simply standing in the way?

"Could you scoot over so Kat can come sit with me?" Ben asked politely.

"What?" Brooklyn looked at me then did an exaggerated double take, like she had no idea I'd been standing there. "Oh, sure. Whatever."

I said nothing, but glanced at her face as I moved around her to sit with Ben. Her eyes were slightly red, and maybe a little watery.

Was Brooklyn Bigelow crying?

She could be a mean girl. She was petty, and underhanded, and a vicious gossip. But she'd also had a pretty bad trip. She'd been exiled from the Satellite Girls, rejected by a boy she liked (who liked her number-one enemy), and had been publicly blamed for the Bathroom Door Mishap. I didn't envy her one bit. But I didn't hate her, either. I did, in fact, feel a tiny bit sorry for her, because Ben liked me and I was feeling charitable.

Just before I sat down, Shoshanna Longbarrow glanced up from her spot in the last row and caught my eye. We looked at each other for a moment, and I looked over at Brooklyn and back at Shoshanna. She held my gaze for a minute.

"Brook, why are you standing there like a doorstop?" Shoshanna asked. "Come sit down, for heaven's sake."

And she gestured toward the empty spot in her row next to Shelby.

Brooklyn got into that seat next to Shelby so fast I could have sworn she'd manipulated time and space and suspended the laws of physics. I wasn't sorry to see her back in the realm of the Satellite Girls. She was probably going to be a lot less of a pain to me now that she had Shoshanna to worship again.

As we approached the WELCOME TO THE UNITED STATES OF AMERICA sign, I sat down next to Ben. When the bus crossed over the border, we were together.

And I'll tell you one other thing. Even though there were no ghosts left on the leprechaun bus, Ben Greenblott slipped his hand into mine.

And I have to say, seeing nothing never looked so good.